The Redirection of Forever

Edward Kane

Stranded Publications

For Aleks—you're still the light despite the darkness.

And to ten-year-old me:
WE DID IT, KID! A book with *your* name on it.
Sorry, it took so long.

Also by Edward Kane

Coming in 2025:

The Pursuit of Shadows

an ongoing dark fantasy/horror series beginning with

three novellas

Contents

The Hummingbird Man

The pier's parking lot was vacant, save for the strands of faded yellow crime scene tape billowing in the breeze. The car grumbled as I turned the ignition key off. It was old and unreliable like the boisterous man I drove by a few miles ago. He stopped me to explain all about a filthy homeless man who gave him a hat to shield him from the elements, then the homeless man vanished into thin air leaving only a thrilled man in a dirty hat. As if a homeless man would give anything to anyone, let alone disappear.

This was not a place where kind things happened. Not anymore.

My eyes cringed at the sound of the creaking car door, and I felt like I was floating over the ground. Being back here hurt... and suddenly, I heard her voice echo through my head. She laughed and said, "That's the understatement of the year."

The pier was overflowing with people that night, she was happy, cackling with laughter. I still see her like that—her head tossed back, laughter like thick smoke. She was impossible to ignore. And as such, few were able to walk by her without making eyes at her.

"Drew! Come on, you know you're more than just the weird boyfriend deterrent."

"Am I? We come to Lover's Ledge and you shoot your eyes all over, like you're baiting any and all."

She turned away from me, and I saw her tense up as she made eye contact with a bulky guy who looked a bit older than us. Anne ran to my side and snuggled against me.

There was shame in her eyes. She was embarrassed that I was right. She started to speak but I put my finger to her lips.

"You don't have to explain. I'm sorry I was so—" I didn't finish the thought because it didn't need to be said. We knew where we stood. We knew no one else would understand and that was okay because...

I felt a twitch rise up my spine and settle in my neck.

Anne and I were best friends since the third grade. My life was at a standstill without her. Twenty years doesn't disappear inside of two.

No one knows why she was dumped here; is it strange that I think maybe it would be different if I had answers.

Everyone I knew had something to say about it. Their words never ceased repeating in my head, ringing like a church bell to an outsider: "She's gone. You have to move on."

Anne was the only one who didn't make me feel like the odd man out. And she's gone. How am I supposed to just be okay?

The chorus continued. "It's been nearly two years. Move on."

As I approached the pier, it was difficult to remember a time when this relic was attractive. She was found below the rickety boardwalk pier that extended outward from the parking lot. The pier was scenic, too high up for fishing but you could stand and feel the pleasant breeze off the ocean. It was a common place for engagements and romantic encounters. Maybe it was that atmosphere that made it appealing. It's definitely the atmosphere now that—

A lone strand of dingy crime scene tape flitted in front of me.

My best friend was stolen from the world and left beneath like common litter. Everyone has given up—moved on—including the police.

I collapsed. My knees collided with the pavement and I groaned heavily. While on the ground, the tears came.

A strange, weary voice flew through the breeze. "If you want to tell him, then you should tell him."

I wiped my eyes and looked toward the sound, not sure if the statement was meant for me or a third party. A dirty brown rag was pressed toward me. I declined the offer, and watched it disappear into a pocket of a long coat. It, too, was old and unraveling. The dark coat gave way to a man with soft eyes and an even softer expression. His hair was cleaner than the rest of him, untouched by the effects of the weather. He reached a hand up toward his head, as if to adjust a hat, then quickly lowered his hand. I saw surprise in his eyes.

"If I offer you my hand, will you take it?"

He sounded eager to help. I nodded and then took his outstretched hand. "Thank you," I croaked.

Once I got to my feet, I stepped backward to brush myself off and then felt guilty for stepping away from him.

He smiled and adjusted his coat's collar. The look on his face didn't match the words he said. "Getting colder."

"Yeah... I wasn't expecting it to be this windy." As soon as I said it, I heard myself saying it to Anne, years before. I closed my eyes and my whole body shivered.

I opened my eyes to find the man standing further from me, with his pointer finger extended and before I could ask what he was pointing at, a tiny hummingbird landed on his finger.

"Whoa!"

The man looked at the bird and nodded once then said, "I can't ask him that."

"Ask me what?"

"No, I meant I don't have to ask."

"What?" The wind was fierce, and I wanted to fall away with it; in that same moment I saw the bird who was holding fast, by looking at the bird I couldn't tell it was incredibly windy. It was unfazed.

"You knew the girl that was found here," The man didn't break eye contact. He stood there with eyes that had no business being as kind as they were.

"Anne. Yeah. She was special. Just knowing she had my back meant the world to me, I felt like none of the day-to-day bullshit had any hold on me because she was there. And I was there for her. Except... when it counted."

The man took a step toward me.

"No, that's not right. You can't do that."

"What?" I winced away from him.

"You can't blame yourself. Her death wasn't your fault."

"It feels like it is," I looked away, back to the car and the bright pink heart sticker still remained on the side next to the rear light. She put it there when I wasn't looking. Now it's faded.

"Do you know how long hummingbirds live?"

I shook my head.

"Less than five years. Most often around three. That's shorter than your time spent in high school."

Flashes of high school fluttered across my vision as if the little bird was doing it, flapping memory after memory at me.

"Let me ask you something, how long has it been since..." He didn't finish. He didn't have to.

"Nearly two—" I choked and couldn't get all the words out.

Clouds rolled in above foretelling a storm, the man brought the bird closer to his chest and said, "The weather's changing."

"I won't be long," I said as I walked past him toward the pier that was roped off with chains and a sign that warned against trespassers. I climbed over it and took a breath. The salt water was like balm for my entire being. The waves crashed below me and I thought of Anne crashing along with the water. It hurt. It hurt so goddamn much.

"What am I supposed to do now? Everyone says to move on. Everyone talks and talks, yet you were the only one that listened. You were the only one I needed and now..." I beat my fists down on the wooden railing. The water had damaged the wood and I felt splinters clash against my skin.

How long ago had the pier been built? It was still here. It was condemned but remained steady and solid. I wiped my eyes and looked back toward the parking lot. The man with the long coat was gone. For a brief moment, I thought I heard a fluttering of wings that seemed to fade into the breeze like a few grains of sand caught in the wind.

The rain began and from more than a hundred feet away, I could see the faded pink sticker on the rear of the car. As I approached, I saw the rain running through the layer of dirt on the car. I smiled.

"Twenty years doesn't disappear inside of two."

A Vast Eulogy

One

Renee Clark grits her teeth, knowing what her mother is about to say from the subtle sobs coating her breathing.

"Renee, honey, you need to come home."

"We've talked about this, Mom." Renee sighs. "Look, okay I know it's not easy to make friends but your daughter can't be your only friend. I need room to breathe and figure out who I am. And you know I don't mean any disrespect, it's just I can't. I'm not capable of mimicking your life, and I don't want to."

"So you're working in the middle of the night behind a glass window that they claim is bulletproof, but we both know they are too cheap to have actual bulletproof glass. What happens when you get robbed and... he has a gun...?"

She hears her mother drop the phone and the unmistakable sobbing, her head resting on the wall that creates the corner of the modest kitchen. The cracked vinyl floor hangs in Renee's mind like an echo. The texture of it and the memories of baking cookies, and sneaking her vegetables to the family dog, Knob.

When her mother brought the puppy home, Renee made a series of sounds and the only one that resembled a word was Knob. She was three at the time. Knob proved to be better than her father but still he couldn't stay.

They say after high school it's all downhill and Renee found that to be true. Four months after graduating, Knob passed away unexpectedly in his sleep. It was a night that was especially hard for her. The longing for her father was strong, and Knob protected her from the nightmares. She knows he took them on and fought for her, yet didn't make it. To this day, Knob remains by her side. She has a tattoo of his paw print on her hip.

After a few moments, she hears her mother pick the phone up. "You're doing what you promised you wouldn't do. You know that, don't you?"

"No. That's not what this is and you know it, Mom. We've talked about this. I'm not Dad. I told you I was leaving. I told you why and how it's only temporary. I promise it is. I just have to find my own path." She can feel the anger rising in her. She wants to scream at her mother, again.

Her mother interrupts. "And you think you're going to find it at that little shit shop?"

"Mom, please." She's trying to keep her voice level. She knows that her mother is just worried, not angry. There's no reason to snap at her. "Mom, look it's late and we both know you need your rest. You'll feel better in the morning. You can call me when you wake up. It'll be like I'm home. We'll sit, have coffee, and chat a little."

"Could we do the zoomies?" Her mother's voice perks up like a child asking for admittance into the cookie jar.

"Yes, of course, Mom. I really have to go. The fog really rolled in, I gotta take it slow on the way to work."

"Okay honey, you be safe. I'll see you in the morning."

"See you later, Mom. I love you."

Her mother returns the sentiment and they click the end call button at the same time. She slides her phone into the front pocket of her hoodie, adjusting it to make sure that it won't slip out. Then she takes her blue and white rectangle name tag and pins it above her left breast. Again, taking the time to make sure it's straight and level. She'll have a total of ten, maybe twelve interactions with people during her six-hour shift, but it's the principle of the thing.

In the bathroom, she brushes her teeth quickly. She swears she did it when she got up, but the mention of her father left a bad taste in her mouth and she couldn't recall exactly if she had brushed or not. The last of the minty fresh toothpaste is exiled from her mouth and she taps her worn out brush on the edge of the sink. Looking in the mirror, she adjusts her tight bun ensuring none of her pesky brown hair has tried to escape.

"Mom really has nothing to worry about. I'm a capable woman." She's thinking of the other night when a young skater punk pointed to the Skateboarding Prohibited sign and began grinding along the curb outside her booth. When she came out the rear door and he saw her standing there, all five feet and ten inches of her, he hauled ass out of there. Just another case of "look at the little lady all safe behind the glass."

She wouldn't say she's a big or imposing girl. She's an athletic twenty-five-year-old, that's all. Athletic. That's the word her boss, Randy, always uses. He's nice and means well, but his mouth doesn't exactly have a filter. He hasn't been rude, only that he says things that she likes to believe most probably wouldn't. It makes her uncomfortable to have to describe people in detail, but Randy, oh no problem at all. He'll give anyone any detail they want and some they don't. There was an instance a few weeks ago where a young college girl hadn't paid for the gas she pumped, and Randy described her down to how her pants fit. "Officer, you know what I'm saying when I say that she had these jeans on that fit squarely. Oh man, the pockets were nicely seated in the center of her plump cheeks." Every adjective gets an exaggerated pronunciation. The policeman didn't favor that sort of talk, but Renee believes it was mostly for her benefit.

She smiles in the mirror, proceeding to roll her neck around before rushing through her one-bedroom apartment; switching lights off as she goes before scooping up her keys, and locking the door behind her. The outside air hits her hard. A push of dense humidity. She likes the first-floor apartment, easy to get in and out of. Though working nights is troublesome since she has to sleep during the day when her upstairs neighbor is doing yoga and other exercises, while her husband is out pretending to work the job he was fired from weeks ago. The lady, Candice, doesn't seem to care about much besides her advanced internet yoga.

The fog lays over her familiar surroundings. It's enough to disorient her but at the same time she's reminded of early mornings as a child—Christmas and the like—when she'd jump in her parent's bed, and they would hide beneath the covers. She would have to grope around to find their heads and hands. She thinks the world is allowed to hide under a blanket whenever it wants, as there's plenty to hide from.

The engine of her early nineties Ford Ranger turns over easily. The shifter sticks so she has to really jerk into drive before releasing the brake and coasting down the hill. She isn't sure why or how she started doing it, but she won't press the gas until the very last second —just before the rising of the hill. She can almost hear her father saying, "Coast whenever possible—saves gas." She slams her hand down on the steering wheel, cursing aloud. Again, punishing herself for thinking of him.

The street rises and turns toward the left before forking outward, there's a light that guards the juncture. Another car approaches from the opposing direction but she manages through the light just as it turns from green to yellow. Now, the road is fixed on another hill that rises deeper into the foggy summer night. A few more twists and bends, and she is entranced by the routine of the drive to work.

She takes her eyes off the road for a split second to hit the radio, bringing it back to life. Ahead of her, a solitary street lamp glows into the night and through the fog illuminating a change in the scenery. A change to the road. It quivers and rises as her truck passes under the lamp. The road has blended with an otherworldly entity. The lamp revealing the entrance into that entity, forming a tunnel.

She doesn't notice the change because she is preoccupied. Even if she was paying attention, she wouldn't believe her eyes.

The road has become a tongue and the street light is the uvula of an entity that doesn't call this world home. It is an intruder and Renee has returned the favor, unaware.

Two

A bright light shines through the windshield, washing Renee's face, and waking her mind from a slumber she doesn't recall entering. Yawn and stretch. "Ah hell! I missed work." She shuffles around for her phone but it's gone. It's not in her pocket. She unbuckles her seat belt and leaps out of the truck, searching under the seat and around the truck.

The ground feels softer than it should. She looks toward her feet and almost falls backward. "Sand. What the—"

The truck is neatly nestled in a small sand dune. One of many that she can see. The view is brilliant. The urge to panic is knocked away by bewilderment. Sand rises and falls, gliding and glittering under a somber blue sky with a falling sun. The light is quietly bright, the kind that speaks of evening to her mind. Morning sunlight is often too loud. This light, early evening light, is more of a soothing light that lets you go about your business. The morning sun is one that makes demands. Often, the demands are awful.

How can anyone say life is awful when there are views like this? She shuts her eyes gently and inhales deeply. Letting the calm take hold of her. There's no use for panic.

She scans the land, looking for some landmark, a destination. The question of how she arrived here doesn't cross her mind, it might later but now she's too enchanted by the view to care about what has happened. She's locked in on what's about to happen.

Quickly, she kicks her sneakers off and tosses them in the bed of the truck. The sand is delightful between her toes. It's warm and fine, not coarse. After a few steps toward the horizon, away from the truck, she reconsiders leaving her sneakers and turns back to scoop them up. Her pointer finger resting in the left and her middle finger holding the right.

A loud crash seems to float through the air toward her. She wonders if it's possible for someone to throw sound because that's what it is like. Seconds later, another crash. It's not thunder, she knows that much. It's something else.

The truck begins to shake and the ground rumbles with it. The sand dunes are shifting around her. Renee tumbles backward and gasps as her truck is swallowed by the sand.

The sunlight is drifting, setting. Renee looks toward the light source and sees it's not setting, it's being hidden. A mountain is forming between her and the sun. The desert goes dark. The mountain is enormous and she knows it's impossible to climb. She has no desire to try, but she's not quite sure how she knows or why she feels this way. It's just something that is not meant to be conquered. It's not sinister, though it is the source of the crashing pulses. She isn't sure how she knows that either.

She wonders if it is trying to speak to her.

The outline of the mountain is beautifully illuminated by the falling sun. She turns around quickly realizing what it is trying to convey—within the clutch of darkness is where she should be focusing. Darkness hides a lot. The light isn't an answer to her query but a distraction.

She looks away from the mountain, squints her eyes and finally is able to see. There is enough light beaming around the mountain to show her that the desert does have an ending. The horizon is shaded like the space between the two pages of an open book. The spine holds it all together. The horizon isn't where the sky ends and the land begins. It's where two ideas fold into each other.

She sees and walks toward the truth.

Land is below your feet and sky is above, she thinks while stepping across the horizon. She has one foot on the sand and one on the sky but the blue sky isn't really what she thought it was.

The sky is an ocean and the sun has fallen behind the solid ground. It shines through the cracks and the crevices. Gravity follows her like a stray dog. She looks back, gazing on the flaws of the solid ground, remembering fondly nights spent staring up at the stars.

"I'm never going to look at the sky the same," she says with a smile, wiggling her toes in the shallow water.

Three

Hours of warm, fine sand grazing and touching her bare feet fade from her mind like a dream that disrupted peaceful sleep. The ocean is cool and refreshing. The feeling of weightlessness is incredible. She releases a tender moan of pleasure and realizes it's been such a long time since she's had any sort of real pleasure. Indulging her desires for true sanity and freedom haven't left room for bodily pleasures or other cathartic releases. Getting one's mind right has to take precedence over physical pleasures.

At least that's what she tells herself when certain cravings arise.

It's better to just say no all the way around than run the risk of repeating her mother's mistakes. Scoundrels like her father are a dime a dozen.

Vigorously, she shakes her head. "Focus on the water. The water. The water. The water..." Her head begins to nod on its own. She has learned to self-hypnotize when the thoughts in her head betray her.

The salt in the water and the air soothes her tongue and nose. After a few moments, she lets her eyes draw open again to soak in the sights. She lets them drift wherever they want to go. There's no need to search for anything. Patience unlocks many doors—locked or otherwise. Waiting isn't the hard part, and neither is the gathering of knowledge. The hard part is staying open to receive it.

The ocean is vast. She chuckles at the thought. Of course it is. The word, ocean, implies that. But it's much more expansive than she thought possible much like the desert. Looking up, she's scanning for a grain of sand or some sign of either the mountain or the desert, but it's just blue. Endless blue.

She wonders if she met with the horizon again if it would fold and let her roll onto the other side. Perhaps this is only a giant fish bowl and all there is to do is swim around in circles, endlessly. No, that's too sinister. This place is alive. I can feel it and I believe it has tried to communicate with me. She's thinking of the pulses in the shadow of the mountain. She walks forward. At least, the direction she believes to be forward. The water does look to deepen ahead...

Four

Renee swims. The water is a clear yet opalescent hue—to call it merely blue would sell it short. And something inside of her worries of offending it. The deeper she goes the more she feels that this whole place is alive. More alive than people she has encountered. Not that a single (and friendless) night cashier can say much about human interaction.

If there was a shred of belief in her of a higher power, then her voice would surely be hoarse by now but it's not. She figures there's no need to yell and scream into the open air when there's much to learn and gain and witness with the sound turned off. Voices are intentional and often accidental weapons.

Her arms begin to tire and, in an instant, she catches a glimpse of something floating in the water. Something large enough to carry her. For a brief moment, she considers the idea of wishes and genies but brushes it off by forgetting her breast stroke in favor of the quicker freestyle motion.

The time it takes her to reach the floating object is there and then gone just as fast. But maybe the passage of time is different here—wherever here is. She dismisses every thought of what the floating object could be before she is able to touch it. Wondering leads to disappointment.

It's a book. A massive hardback with a tattered spine. Can books float? She wonders as she climbs on top of it. It's coarse. Almost like sand, she thinks. Recalling her time in the desert, she wonders if she'll ever find a way out of here.

Five

Her life raft rattles her awake. She shakes her head, not remembering when or how she fell asleep. The thought to question how long it's been strikes her, but fades quickly when she sees what stirred her awake.

The shore.

The book scrapes along the surface like coarse sand paper on bone. For a brief moment she can taste the desert and a bubble of fear expands in her. She lets her feet to the ground. It's not sand!

A gorgeous burnt orange cobblestone pathway unrolls in front of her. Trees line either side of the pathway before her, springing up suddenly along both sides of the path. A forest of dead trees. There are no leaves. Only the cold grayed out color of death. Whatever lies ahead is not happy, nor will it be lively.

To her surprise, she's wishing for the warm welcoming golden glow of the desert. She thinks herself odd because there was only emptiness there. Here there is variety, personality. Even if the personality is a friend to the grim reaper.

Something draws her further along the path—it's a feeling, a semblance of purpose. She focuses on the path, unable to make heads or tails of how she feels exactly. The cool cobblestones are refreshing on her bare feet, but also there's a pang of horror in each step. Then she sees it.

Maybe fifteen paces in front of her is a stone fountain. At first, she swears there is water running down along the edge of the circular basin at the top, but she blinks and sees it is empty.

The cooling sensation of the cobblestones is the same as the ocean because the ocean began as the water that flowed through this fountain. Her head snaps, looking back the way she's come. She gasps and turns back to notice the break in the wall that surrounds the dead fountain.

The stone broke away and birthed the ocean.

The demolished fountain is an enchanting white green, from this distance she can't tell if it's meant to be that color or if there's mold or fungus growing and contaminating the color. Before she can plant her foot, completing another step, a dark shape flickers into view. It's shaped like the mountain, only smaller. A soft triangle of total darkness. She manages to exhale and plant her foot on the cobblestone path.

The dark shape turns toward her.

It's a silhouette of a man. He's hunched over. There's no skin that she can see, but he is sitting on the edge of the fountain wall. She feels a pulse not unlike the one the desert mountain sent her way. It's communication.

Whatever this dark figure is, it's trying to communicate with me. She swallows hard when the thought completes in her mind. Renee straightens her own spine, in opposition of what she sees in front of her and clears her throat.

"Can you... understand me?" She forces the words out despite the quaking she feels in every fiber of her.

The shape flickers and two eyes emerge. They are gold and brilliant and beautiful. The dark figure seems to nod in response to her question.

"Can you speak? Like me, I mean. Before you were trying, I think. Am I correct?" Her hands are trembling uncontrollably now.

"Yes. Correct. You, Renee, are correct." The voice is thick, the sound is like the mixing of cement. Loud, too. But still unsure. They are both unsure of each other and their ability to speak.

"Where are we?" She asks, pushing each word out with an immense amount of force.

"Me." The figure brings a long hand with skinny fingers up toward its head and points at its own temple.

Renee shakes her head. "I don't understand."

It puts its hands to its chest. "This is not... me." The figure seems to struggle with the word me or maybe just the idea of self. It stretches its arms outward. "All this is... me."

"You're saying." She stops. "You're saying that all of this is you. I'm inside... of you? How is that possible? What are you? Am I dead?"

The figure shakes its head. "No, I am. You came into me through my spreading weakness."

She closes her eyes. The sound and the sensation of a headache grinds and shakes on her mind like a train on old tracks. The dark road on the way to work returns to her mind. And the fog. She sees the fog and what she didn't see prior to waking up in the desert.

"You swallowed me up." In her mind, she fantasizes about losing her grip in this moment and letting whatever it is really have it. The anger and the pain and fear are all there, bubbling inside her. She could let it all out but something tells her that it would accomplish nothing. And this being, whatever it might be is not deserving of it. For all she knows, it yawned and she drove into the open mouth without even knowing.

"You should sit. I am learning your communication through your thinking mind. In a moment, we will continue."

Still wary of this being in front of her, she sits on the opposite end of the break in the fountain wall. "It must have been beautiful. How did it break?"

"I told you. I am dying."

Six

Shifting her legs into her preferred crossed position, she feels the fountain crumbling beneath her. Renee stumbles. A hand reaches down into her view and she takes it. She looks up into the man's pale blue eyes. "You... changed?" She barely manages to push the words off of her tongue.

"Yes. I learned it would be easier to talk like this. However..." He stops and looks out the way she came.

She follows his gaze. The enchanting path of cobblestones has mysteriously vanished.

"How is it all gone?"

"I told you. I am dying." He turns away and looks back. His returning glance peers deeper into her eyes. "Can you see in my eyes?"

"See what?"

"My eyes. I cannot tell or see if you are seeing in my eyes."

"How can you not?"

"Because this is not me. It is only for you."

"So, all of this, this... was what? A journey through your mind? What are you?"

"Not only my mind. You are in me. I have never met a being that did not understand me already, so I do not know how to begin to describe."

"Where are you from?" Renee feels like a child approaching an animal at a zoo for the first time. "What should I call you?"

"I was not born or birthed like you humans are. I have just been, and now I am dying. Does it matter what you call me since soon I will be gone?"

"How can you die if you were not born? Doesn't one need the other?"

"In human terms, yes. I am not human and I don't know that we can relate like you expect or desire to."

"If that's true then why would you try and try and try to talk to me?"

He replies with only silence. So, she speaks again, "I think every living thing at one time or another desires some sort of connection even if we don't know it."

"You speak the words and I see they ring true inside your heart."

"What?"

"You are unaware that you speak of yourself in this moment. You are projecting yourself on to me."

Her arms go limp and she just stands there, essentially lifeless.

"Renee? Did I break you with your own truth?" He reaches his hand out to touch her shoulder. "You think that you came here to find and help me, but maybe you found your way into me so I could help you."

"Do I... do you think I need help?"

"I think you felt at home here because you're used to feeling lost. Somehow you have made it so lost is safe for you."

She collapses. Falling into his arms.

Seven

Renee lifts her head, expecting to gaze into the enchanting eyes of a creature that has her captive in every sense of the word. But he's not there. He's gone. She knows that only the vision of the brown skinned man he was pretending to be is gone, though the clanging empty sound pounds every ounce of her.

Her mouth opens and she realizes that, again, she has nothing to say. The silence says it all.

Eight

"What happens now?" She finally asks into the emptiness. A few seconds drag through her mind and corner her patience. "Is it possible for me to return to Earth?"

A roll of thunder or something like it fills the emptiness. "You are from the Sacred Earth?"

"Sacred? I don't know. But I am from Earth. I live in Rhode Island, grew up in New Hampshire."

"Renee, you are from the Sacred Earth. I understand."

The excited tone of its voice is unmistakable.

"What do you understand? Did you have a question before?" She's panting the words out—a rapid exhaust of syllables.

"I did not understand how we came in contact exactly, but would you care to hear a story?"

She nods, understanding that the odd segue is only odd to her. This place is an infinite labyrinth that belongs to something far greater than anything humanity has to offer. The thought completes itself in her mind and she feels a pang of guilt. This being would not agree with her on this. How she knows this is a mystery to her.

"I do not know a word to describe what I am. I like the word I have found in your thoughts—vast. It is simple yet grand. It fits me, I believe. I am not the only one, but we are not as many as you—as humanity. But you have family, I do not. There are places like Sacred Earth that are quite mythical. Stories are important, no matter what. When I was not quite as expansive as I am, a fellow Vast—one that would force you to find a different word for us—spoke of Sacred Earth and the human plague. That is the word it spoke; it is not mine. Grand Vast, I shall call it that because I find it to be fitting, spoke of war and violence and things I could not fathom, and it spoke of weakness, of love. The more Grand Vast spoke, the more I found my thoughts drifting from that perspective into an alternate view. I was infatuated. And I remain so.

"When the Vast learn or sense of their expiration they are permitted to sway. And many sway to find out if the myths their Grand Vasts spoke of are true. That was what I was doing, but I remember coming into a fog and being confused like how you wake from your nightmares of your father. I am sorry for saying so, but I have begun to think it terrible of me for not mentioning."

The voice stops.

She is swallowed by the idea of something watching her dreams and this emptiness she's trapped in. "Please. Do not stop speaking. The empty..."

"Do you want to find him?"

Renee shakes her head. Then stops herself. "I... I'm not sure. I hate thinking of him. I really really hate it. And I don't want to hate anything. I don't want to be my mother but I love her so much. It wouldn't be so bad to be just like her. I just... I just want more. Because I know as bad as I feel about him, she feels even worse, but at the same time she loves me so it's not like she can totally hate him. Ugh! You must think humanity is..." She stops, trying to find the right word but settles for only a shrug.

"No, Renee, I do not think humanity is terrible. On the contrary, I am honored to have found you."

"You are? I don't think I understand."

"You proved me right, Renee."

Nine

Opalescent eyes appear in the blanket of blank space surrounding her. Part of her thinks she should be afraid, but another part knows that at this point fear will get her nowhere.

She thinks about the Vast's words. She's not sure she likes the word as a title for it but she understands it's not up to her. Not exactly, anyway. She can't quite grasp the idea that she will go on living after this. Part of her believes this to be the test before her final resting place is decided. And she wonders if it, the Vast, can hear her thoughts.

"Yes," The voice of the Vast bellows from everywhere and nowhere. "You believe in an afterlife, Renee?"

"I'd like to. There's no reason to swear it off and claim that this, I mean Earth, is all there is. But I don't know what I'd expect from it or if I imagine it any certain way. I suppose it's like a dark room or house. I know that there is something in that darkness but it's unknown to me until the place is illuminated. I'm curious, but not curious enough to rummage around for a light switch."

"But you think this might be a test?"

"It's possible, that's all, I think. On Earth there is the common heaven and hell idea, the good versus the bad. Good people go to the clouds and bad people go to the flames."

"You do not like this idea?"

"I think that if there was some supreme being that it would be much more complex than just 'okay you this way and you this way. Good up, bad down.'"

The being laughs. It's an awful nasally sound, not far from wheezing.

"Are you... laughing?" She asks warily.

"Can you not see the comedy?"

She can only shake her head in response to the question. Her fears grip her tongue tightly.

"You and I both have these ideas about so-called myths that have been told to us. We are each other's confirmations."

Renee considers this for a moment and then she too, laughs.

Ten

"I need to apologize to you, Renee."

"What for?"

"I abandoned a question of yours. I did not mean for this. Do you accept my apology?"

She shifts her weight, as if to brace herself. "What question did you skip over?"

"You asked if it is possible for you to return to Earth. I was taken... away by your mention of Sacred Earth." The Vast's voice trails off. Then picks up again, "I want to answer your question but, I also do not."

"I don't understand."

"If I answer it then I have to watch you leave. But if I do not answer and there is a hell... I have never enjoyed heat."

"What about the desert?"

"That is a result of dying. I do not recall what it was before but I know it was beautiful. I know that dying, for my kind, is a process of eliminating beauty. I suppose letting you go is the final piece."

Eleven

Renee closes her eyes and thinks of climbing the mountain. She's not sure she can make it but the Vast believes in her. And that does count for something.

To hear it talk of the final piece... she hopes she never has to endure anything like that again. Let alone remember it clearly.

The details of its finality are difficult for her to process. Somehow, she will make it out of here, out of the Vast, when she reaches the top of the mountain.

"Tell me, where will you go when I... when you leave?" There's a cautious note to the voice of the Vast.

"Will it be the same time as it was when I..."

"I do not know. I think it will be later."

"I have to have coffee with my mother. If there's time a nap would be nice, I guess. Will you... will you die as soon as I make it to the top?" A tear runs down each cheek. She turns around, then realizes she can't hide from the Vast.

"Save your tears. They are your way home."

She nods, understanding that the Vast says more when it surrounds her with silence. It overwhelmed her before but now she understands this being, as much as her humanity will allow.

The eyes in the blankness become a mountain before her. She gazes at the slope which is softer than the one of the mountain she saw previously. It would be possible to run up this one, she thinks, but promises herself not to try it. It is still rugged terrain regardless of the slope.

Renee sees the mountain and immediately understands how the Vast shaped it just for her. It heard her fears and once again she's overwhelmed. But she must save her tears for the summit.

Twelve

Her knees are skinned. The silence has burrowed into her ears and transformed into a terrible droning ache in her head. Her right hand bears a nasty gash that will not heal this month. But here she is.

The summit of the Vast's mountain.

She circles on her heels, ignoring the bitter pain, taking in the full view. The blank space doesn't feel the way it did before. She has filled it. She looks down at her hand, knowing that she shook the hand of something greater than herself. But at the same time, it's not about the better or the lesser—it's about the commonality.

The idea of riding her tears home suddenly makes sense, through the death of this entity she sees and hears the emptiness that she's trying to fill or fix. She says aloud, "The commonality. We have the same hole. We can mend it together."

The tears well and flow forming the only farewell that needs saying. There's more in these droplets than a library of books could say. She knows it. Therefore, the Vast knows it.

Thirteen

Her eyes open.

She's sitting in her truck and in front of her a familiar face stares back. A faded pink pig face—her mother's mailbox. Renee bought it as a Mother's Day gift over a decade ago. The awkward faded thing makes her smile. She remembers telling her mother that every time she opens the mailbox she must oink. Renee wonders if she still complies with the instruction.

Through the open window, she hears voices nearby.

"Krystle, ain't that your daughter's truck?" Curtis Anderson, the elderly fellow from two doors down, shouts as he makes his way from Renee's mom's porch. He likes to bring the paper to the door. Good for his joints and blood flow, he says.

Renee hops out of the truck, slamming the door too loudly. The front door of the house opens. She's standing there in her fleece robe like she knew Renee would come instead of call. Like something told her to be ready.

Curtis chuckles and continues his way to the next yard, collecting another neighbor's paper for express delivery.

Renee runs to her mother, dropping her keys along the way. Her tears are flowing like rolling river rapids. She grips her mother in a hug unlike any other they've shared. Renee feels reassured when she can feel her mother's tears flowing like her own.

"I'm glad you're my mom, mom. And I'm sorry for making you feel any different."

"Nonsense, dear. Let's get you inside. There's coffee, you know." Her mother blossoms brightly and pushes her daughter to the door. She gazes over to the truck, and the trail in Renee's wake. "What's with all the sand?"

Warm Anchors

Jason watched a middle-aged man of Asian descent, maybe Indian, scratch frantically at his leg before lifting his pant leg to get the itch more directly. The man didn't seem to notice or care about an unusual horseshoe shaped lump or scar—Jason wasn't sure which would be the right term. The airport, for some reason he thought he was in Vienna, wasn't crowded but there were plenty of people, too many for Jason's liking. He wanted to get up and walk away but that wasn't possible. He wasn't going to move because he couldn't.

He felt it on his skin then. Not his leg but his forearm, left to be exact—which worked out because he was right-handed and could scratch the bastard out of this world. The urge told him he could scratch it and it'd be all better. When he tried, he was unable. He couldn't move his arms or his eyes.

He was transfixed on this man and his family—two young children. The man, presumably the father, was the only one with a horseshoe shaped scar. He had been poisoned; Jason felt he knew the security camera footage would prove him correct.

These feelings made no sense like the logic in a dream but he was here, somehow, yet an immovable observer.

A loud voice screeched through speakers above and all around him. He blinked his eyes and allowed his mind to take in what he was seeing.

He was not in Vienna. He was not watching a deadly virus being unleashed and framed around an innocent family.

He was freaking out, again. This was only the latest scenario.

He knew it was only a matter of time until the next. He didn't feel fear. Because when they came, he was already gone. Who he was faded and he became a sort of narrator of these stories, an observer. When the scenario came to him, as the horseshoe shape had, and related itself to him then he would snap out of it. In the back of his mind was a fear that a scenario would come along and not feature a reminder of his own humanity. Something alien, something outside of what his empathy was capable of.

Jason looked around in search of an anchor. He need-ed something to reestablish where he was, and more importantly who he was. He knew his name, he always had that immediately but beyond that, nothing.

A voice came across a speaker above his head. It was a message to someone with a name that sounded of Asian heritage, the voice wanted the person to report to a specific gate, as their plane was about to take off. He understood then where he was and where the scenario came from. His mind was deeply affected by what was around him which was why he did his best to keep to his familiar surroundings. This scenario was huge because he left his home. And from the look of his current whereabouts, he made it through airport security and was about to board a plane. That's what triggered his anxiety.

He looked down at his lap and saw the boarding pass secure in his wallet, which he was holding along with his banged-up iPhone 4 that actually wasn't his but it had been in the lost and found for over six months that he knew of. At this point, who would claim a phone that old?

Another message came across the PA system, alerting all to the baggage policy and if anyone who finds unattended bags to notify Boston PD or Logan International Airport security.

Boston, he was in Boston.

Jason looked at his boarding pass which listed Delta as flight carrier and Las Vegas as his destination. He had no business going to Vegas. What the hell was he going to do in Vegas? He could hear it off in the distance, approaching fast, another scenario. Another fit of anxiety.

A different sound interrupted the terrible train in his mind. It was the sound of barking from a mid-sized dog. He whipped his head toward the sound and he was awarded the sight of a brown pup running toward him, leash dragging along the floor. Jason bent down in time to receive the animal who bounded into his arms. He could tell it was a mix of sorts but what most people were seeing was a pit-bull. This pup had the face of a pit and what a beautiful face it was. To everyone around Jason, though, it was something to fear.

"Damnit Win!" A woman short of breath said as she came upon Jason and the dog. She put her hands to her knees and bent over, in an effort to catch her breath.

She was a bit over five feet tall, maybe five six with average heels on. Her hair brown with a hint of faded color, maybe purple or red, it had been a while and though her hair was disheveled, it was a fixed chaos in a messy bun. The red and white messenger bag on her shoulder knocked against her, almost toppling her from its weight as she knelt down to pet the dog.

"She never is like this with strangers," the girl said looking at Jason who then met her gaze.

He cracked a bashful smile, "What's her name?"

"Winston. I call her Win. I know, I know. Boy's name but it was what came to me when I first saw her at the shelter. Her little ears perked up when I called her Winston."

"Can't argue with those ears," Jason said while rubbing the sides of the dog's head and ears.

"I'm glad she came to you rather than," She motioned her head to the crowd forming around. Then her face changed to worry, "Are you okay?"

Jason looked at her and tried to smile but the gesture was forced and he knew it. The smile came and he bit his lip to put it back again. "I, uh. I don't know."

"Dogs are a good judge of character, so you must be an okay guy. It's okay if you're not doing okay. I've said okay way too much now. I'm sorry. I'm Maja." She smiled and ended hers with an upward blow of air through her lips to push away the stray strand of hair that came loose from her bun.

He smiled at her. It came effortlessly and at first, he didn't even know it was happening but when he did, he tried to kill it and stop it from reaching her sight line. It was too late. She saw and he tried to fight the smile. She reached for his hand then. Weakly, he said, "My name's Jason."

"It's nice to meet you, Jason. Win and I were supposed to get on another flight but we've decided to stay here in Boston. Where you off to?"

A soft chuckle pursed his lips. "About the same, actually."

"Oh yeah?"

"Mhmm, I don't know why I came to the airport," He swallowed hard.

"Neither does Win! Come on, let's get out of here. I feel like they are gonna stare holes through me."

His eyes dart around the large opening of a room that seemingly goes on forever. They call them gates but they are exits from this expanse. He can feel all their eyes. Every single staring eye.

He can't blink because if he does then they will close in on him.

***

All that could be heard was large pounding wings. Followed by a terrible screech that shattered glass and sent chills up every spine in the vicinity. Then the beating stopped and everything shook. The screeching thing was pounding and climbing the concrete sides of the parking structure. Chunks of it clamored between the creature's movements. Voices were calling and screaming but nothing was louder than the thing. It came from above and must have hurt its wings because it was climbing the parking garage, slowly and meticulously. Perhaps in search of something or someone.

Jason felt his feet move forward, one after the other. With each movement, he could feel the urge to look grow stronger while inside he felt more and more confident.

He was observing himself.

He knew this had to be a scenario but that couldn't be because it'd never been like this before. But he was aware of what he was seeing while still seeing it.

He watched his body stop at the edge of the parking structure. He looked outward and saw that in the distance, people were watching. They were too close. The thing on the side of the building could turn and attempt to fly again and destroy them all. Part of him wished it would.

A larger part of him wanted it to stop moving so he could look upon it and learn from it.

Learn what? He wasn't sure, but he was sure there was something to learn.

He heard his name being called and he felt something on his shoulder but he couldn't bring himself to follow those feelings, he had to look over the edge. He had to see what was screeching and causing so much panic.

Jason began to lean towards the edge and the grip on his shoulder tightened, and with it came a feeling around his legs and ankles. He knew what it was but he couldn't put words to it. The sound from below grew louder and more forceful. Time was running out. If he didn't look now then the thing would move and that would be it.

He wasn't sure what that meant but he came this far, he had to know what the thing had for him. Surely, it would be one tiny scrap of something before an untimely painful death. Jason closed his eyes and he could see the fangs. He could see them tearing through him. Then the sensation flooded his whole body. He gasped for breath and with his last shred of energy he pushed himself forward, toes hanging over the edge.

His eyes exploded when they gazed upon the large black bat below. It had fangs taller than Jason and when the thing screeched, Jason felt his hair move and his face moisten. He heard his most recent boss inside of the screech, and he realized then that this was his escape. The way out of his life. The way out of the terrible existence he crafted around the scenarios. He blinked and saw each scenario for what they were: bars of his cell.

He imprisoned himself.

He smiled in the knowledge that he just set himself free.

The bat lifted one of its limbs and it became a twisted black hand. It was impossible. Bats don't have hands.

Jason yelled and the creature below bellowed. The resulting sound was terrible. Two separate entities crying out for life. Then, Jason felt two things at his back. The hand he felt before grabbed at the hood of his sweatshirt and something else yanked at his pant leg. Both pulled at the command of a voice that hollered, "PULL!"

A woman's voice. Jason looked over his shoulder and saw her there, fear in her eyes. Maja. Her messy bun had given out and her hair was all over the place, blowing in the breeze.

"We got you," she said.

He let them have him—the lady and her dog. The truth quickly came to focus as the three fell backward onto the hard surface of the parking structure's roof.

There was no bat. There was only him and the desire for something else which drove him to the edge of a tall building.

"Maja," he said. "I need help."

She held him, and without a word they laid on the cold roof.

***

Jason and Maja settled into an apartment in Westerly, Rhode Island right around the corner from the train station. She needed a quick connection to anywhere and everywhere. While Jason needed quiet, peaceful surroundings. They take Winston for walks in Wilcox Park, and every time they leave the park with new fans. It had been about a year since the airport, since the three of them met and bonded atop the parking garage.

Maja proved to be the perfect anchor for Jason. No episodes in months. His new doctor advised him to stop using the word scenario and Maja agreed. She helped him more than he thought he could be helped but in the corners of his mind...

The doctor told him he can't worry about what might happen. He has to look at what has happened. And take that as proof that he can overcome his problems.

Often, Jason has found himself in a moment seemingly out of time, and in that silence and stoppage all there is, is the way Maja makes him feel and the way she looks at him. He's thought about running but he can't figure out why. He's thought about trying to prolong that feeling of being outside of time. He can't figure out why these ideas come and toss themselves around his mind.

She has done so much for him. It has never ceased to amaze him. More than that, he never stopped feeling like he wasn't worthy of any of it. He began to worry endlessly about it. Somewhere inside he knew it was a problem but he couldn't vocalize it. To put words to it and speak them aloud felt wrong like doing it would unleash something he wouldn't be able to contain. For example, an incredibly large winged creature bent on destruction and death.

There was no filter that told him creatures like that don't exist. The thought took root and it grew in the back of his mind.

One night, the three of them were on the sofa, it was a battered old thing they got secondhand. Jason thought it was clearly it was on at least its third, maybe fourth hand. Maja chose to see it as a feature, like the thing was well loved and not overused. Jason remained on unemployment because they both agreed it wasn't time for him to try to join the workforce. She was exhausted and he knew it. They never really talked about it. And nights like this one, Jason was unable to recall what she did for work. His mind was preoccupied with thoughts of how to push her away. Because when he looked into those tired eyes, he knew she deserved much better. He was foolish to believe that she did not realize those thoughts were on his mind.

They were loud and pressed outward from his eyes as if they were high beams of an approaching car.

Her eyes pulled him in and something clicked. It all just fit.

Suddenly, he saw himself fall off of the parking structure into the mouth of the bat and then everything faded to black. He didn't feel the fangs nor did his skin burst with horseshoe scars. There was a warmth from somewhere and he reached out in search of it. A small sound pierced the darkness and he had his hands around it. The warmth of it was glorious. It was better than sunlight on bare skin. It was better than anything he thought was possible.

And then he realized that it was a scenario. It had to be one. The heat began to intensify and it came upon his own flesh like ocean waves. It rode up his arms and tickled his hair.

A new sound made its way through the pleasant fog he was in. This sound was terrible and threatening. A growl. Jason turned his head toward it and the room came back into focus.

Winston was growling at him, not in the playful way she would when they played tug of war. This was Winston in battle stance. She was giving him one chance to let go or be destroyed. There was anger and power in those eyes. Jason then realized what the warmth was. Slowly his eyes made their way to his hands as he felt his fingers unfurl from Maja's neck.

He swallowed a scream as he stumbled backward. He tried to speak but nothing came. He wanted to apologize to say anything really but like her, he was short of breath. His hand marks remained on her throat. That was when he realized she hadn't moved.

Everything in him sank. He killed her. His skin went cold and he shivered. Behind him, Winston hadn't moved either. Jason looked down at the dog who had her head low. She nudged him toward Maja. He knew that the dog could and had picked up on what he was feeling. She understood as best her dog brain would allow and somehow, she'd already forgiven him.

How, he had no idea because he was doubtful that he'd ever forgive himself. He knelt at Maja's feet and put his hand on her knee. He whispered her name, but she didn't budge. Moving his hand to her face and then her shoulder he tried to rattle her awake but it was no use. He couldn't be gentle at a time like this. Tears streamed down his face as he put his head to her chest, hoping for a pulse. Didn't matter how faint. A pulse is a pulse.

As if summoned, there it was.

His head pressed against her chest; he could hear a faint heartbeat. Like a tapping foot from a great distance. He wasn't sure if a tapping foot could be heard from far but that wasn't the point.

She was alive.

Win nudged at Maja's legs but she did not move. He looked into her face, at her slitted eyes and he said, "Please. Wake up. I don't know what to do. If I call 911—"

Her hand moved and touched him. He leaned back and her hand reached his as her eyes opened a sliver more than before. She shook her head.

"No, I don't... just no."

"You don't want me to get into trouble?" He said through teary eyes and choked throat.

She tried to smile and almost accomplished the feat. "I'll be fine," her words were interrupted by quickened breathing.

"I'm no good for you," he took her hand away from his and stood.

"You... you're gonna leave me like this," she gestured at herself.

A moment passed between them as he thought it over. He thought about how she stood by him through all the shit he brought upon them. From a suicide attempt the day they met to all sorts of crazy stories and arguments over doctors. He looked at her and those eyes cut through him, the way paper can cut through skin—quick and the sting comes later. Her eyes told him everything he needed, but he still wanted to hear her say the words he thought he was picking up from her look.

He sat down beside her and put his hand in hers. Their eyes met and he said, "When you're able. We will talk. Until then, we'll just sit."

She smiled her best and snuggled against him. But he picked her head up and told her that she needed to stay awake because of the possible concussion. And she told him that she would be fine. Though she didn't say how she knew.

About an hour later, she cleared her throat and said his name.

Jason looked at her and then they turned to face each other, they sat with their legs curled in on themselves like pretzels.

"Are you going to ask me?" Maja turned her head, the way she always did. The way he always loved.

"I don't know what question you're referring to."

She groaned, "Okay then tell me what you were thinking about before."

"I don't understand."

"What?" She exhaled, trying to vent the anger.

"No, no, I mean I don't understand why you'd want me to stay."

She raised her voice, "I didn't pull you from that ledge so you could just walk away!"

"What does that mean? Am I your property because you saved my life?"

She threw her hands up and got up from the couch, almost stepping on Winston who lay at the edge of the sofa. She apologized to the dog and looked up at Jason. "What is it you want?"

He shook his head, "I don't—"

"Stop. Don't say that again. Enough. Tell me what you want."

He bit his lower lip and let the question make its way through his mind like a car with one headlight through a dark tunnel. "I want to be better and I thought I was doing a lot better. Clearly, I'm not."

She cringed as if his words hit her as an insult. She knelt down in front of him and put her hands on his knees. "One incident doesn't erase all the progress. You have to know that."

"Maja, why are you being so nice to me? I just about strangled you." Jason turned away from her eyes, unable to face her when he said those words.

"If you want me, really want me, to leave then I will. You have to say it and mean it."

He squeezed her hands then and said, "I don't want you to leave. I think I'm supposed to."

"How is that any different? You or me."

"I look at you and see my hands around your neck. I should go."

"Jason," Her voice became stricter and she gripped the sides of his face. "What do you think I see? You really think that I don't see you on that ledge every single day? Every day I worry about you. Every time I can't see you or hear you, I worry where you are. I told you I'm fine and I mean it. Nothing has changed."

"How can you say nothing has changed?"

Still holding his face, she repeated the sentiment, though slower. "Because nothing has. Jason, you have to listen to what I'm saying and put your own thoughts to the side. Right now, you have to decide if you want to stay and keep trying. Because..." She swallowed and smiled, "I'm in love with you, Jason." Her hands fell from his face and the words seemed to hang in the room like thick morning fog.

Jason looked deep into her eyes and he saw that she was being honest. It didn't make any sense to him. He had come close to killing her and here she was professing her love to him. They hadn't said those words before, but he thought they both did love each other. It was unspoken. And now it wasn't. His immediate instinct was to blurt out the words back to her but she'd see through that. And he'd feel terrible about that.

"It's fresh. I won't be able to not feel guilty."

"Hey, I'm not asking you to not feel bad. You can and should feel but you're not alone. Okay?"

He nodded. "Maja?"

"What is it?"

"I love you, baby."

They shared a kiss and when they pulled away from it, he looked at her and felt strangely. "I don't know how to not feel unworthy of you. Maybe I'd feel better if I understood why."

"Why what?"

"Why me?"

"Love is permission to be irrational. Everyone needs a little crazy. That's what love is."

"My crazy isn't enough?"

"You're not crazy, Jason. No one is crazy. No one is normal. You may think you're the only one but I promise that's not the case."

His face changed, surprised by her comment. "What does that mean?"

"Here, take my hands and close your eyes. I want to tell you the scenario I have seen."

Shock overtook his face, and she had to take his hands, as he closed his eyes. Unable to get the words out of his head until she started speaking.

"I see Win with a bow tied around her dopey head, a basket in her mouth and everyone around us gasping as she almost loses the treasures in it. You're standing there, the smile on your face is bigger than any other you've worn. You're watching us walk down the aisle to you. The dork even joins us in our I Do's. Can you hear her barking after we've said ours?"

He had to open his eyes then because he felt the tears may drown his eyes. If such a thing was even possible. When he opened them and found her crying too. She smiled, showing only a fraction of her teeth, in the way she always did. They embraced and a warmth grew in his heart then.

A warmth from deep within him.

She showed him such a thing was possible.

Across from Starship Central

Cities are supposed to be rich with possibilities, and like the busted street lights, I was once lit with ambition. Power doesn't flow through like it used to. History has crumbled around me, and all I have is the cough from the dust that the ancient buildings left as they collapsed. Often, I mistake the humming of the frequent engine tests as proof that the city is still alive. I've seen the hover trains slow down as they pass through, but I have no idea why. There's not much reason to slow down—I haven't seen anyone in weeks. Haven't even seen myself.

I spend most days traveling between the vacant buildings, despite knowing that less and less are safe. Shoddy construction has finally caught up with them. The buildings creak and groan and some have coughed back at me.

There is one I trust, my last true safe haven. A two-story anchor on one of the two streets that at one time were the pinnacle of this area. It doesn't look like much these days, especially after I gutted the apartments upstairs and set fire to the furniture in the street. Too much weight on the upper floor would eventually ruin the lower, and I couldn't bear this place to be reduced to rubble.

As I walked to my safe haven, the mid-day sunlight felt like an enemy, beating on me as soon as it saw me. Or perhaps it was mocking me. Either way, soon I'd be out of its range. It can't mock me if I can't see it.

As I approached my destination, I allowed myself to remember what it was like: the pictures and displays in the window like an all clear, telling me it was safe to come in.

You're welcome here.

The glass door still featured a hand drawn PULL sign, the penmanship sloppy like the person who wrote it was nervous about such a performance. Even in the summer, the handle was cold. Inside, it smelled of books. So many books. So many kinds of paper, some old and some new just like the clientele.

There was no way that going into outer space would feel even slightly like how I felt in here. A small part of a huge universe—one among many worlds.

I inhaled and the reality of the room came through me. All I had to do was hold the door handle and be transported into my memory of the place.

The once filled book shop was emptied out. All that remained were the dust bunnies, a few free-standing shelves, shards of discolored glass that once made up a case that housed the most expensive trinkets, and last but not least, one lonely spinner rack. The thing creaked and hardly spun. The sound was nearly enough to transport me, but the musty air did it in.

The place was more like an unoccupied basement, in need of a good dusting, but it was safe. The face of the storefront no longer spoke to anything but emptiness. The sign had faded beyond recognition long ago. Longer than I care to admit.

The engines across the river roared to their full volume.

Everything happened in the distance.

I sat there, beside the creaky spinner rack until the day faded and the noise across the river grew. Noise ordinances were things of the past. This city was nothing, especially after it had been picked clean by the recruiters. I declined their advances so often that I had a reputation. It was enough to keep everyone away from me. But now, I'm the ghost haunting these streets.

Some days I'm not even sure I'm alive.

I stood and made my way toward the pier; it was three blocks from the store. The pier was where ferries and ships of all kinds came and docked; sometimes the city would use the pier to host festivals and carnivals. Unfortunately, those days were only remembered by ghosts. I remember some talked fondly of the history of this city, as at one time it was a vital port but I never saw its importance.

My hands held the rusted steel of the railing along one of the only sections of the pier that remained intact. Much of it was collapsed, some from age and others from failed launches. I knew it was only a matter of time before they realized that the abandoned city across from starship central could be demolished and used as a launching bay. They could cut out the need for transporting the starships and just fire people off into the sky from here.

The clattering of a fast-moving train stole my attention. I saw the blur of it coming from the east—people or supplies. Perhaps both.

My eyes shifted and squinted at something strange approaching from the direction I had come. Dim but unmistakable—headlights. I pushed my backside off the railing and stepped toward the street. My feet started without my full awareness. The train and the headlights were fast approaching from opposite angles, and then I realized they were on a collision course.

I hustled over to the section of the tracks that were passable by car, right where the train station was. It was a sad excuse for a train station, but it was where the trains stopped and there was a window where tickets were sold. Surely, it did the job.

When I approached the tracks, I heard a panicked voice calling for help.

"Please! The door is stuck."

The car was a pile of junk on wheels, pieced together from spare parts. Inside I saw a woman struggling at the driver's door. She was heaving herself at the door, perhaps the door handle didn't work. I came around the side and saw the passenger side was welded shut.

I yelled, "The window! Go through the window."

She looked in the direction of my voice.

"Hurry!" I said as I ran the rest of the way and helped her wiggle the whole way out. As she fell out of the car, she collapsed onto me. I heard my ankle crack and the pain shot up through to my knee.

I looked at her, groaning in pain. She wouldn't help a ghost. Whatever she came to do was more important. I could tell from the way she held herself. Her heavy boots spoke multitudes to me. They were boots of a warrior.

Then I saw her stop. I held my breath.

She turned around and looked into my eyes.

I couldn't blink. I couldn't move.

The way she rolled her eyes was nearly audible.

When she leaned down, she cleared her throat—twice—before speaking, "Can you stand?"

I shook my head.

She picked me up and draped my arm around her shoulder. We hobbled away from the tracks in a hurry which made my body hurt more. She told me to shut up. Her voice was gruff. I could tell she meant it.

When the train collided with the car, she didn't look back, and even if I had wanted to, I wouldn't have been able. The sound it made was louder than anything I'd ever heard. I can't imagine that the car survived and surely the train was derailed. There was splashing, indicating some pieces of something made it into the water. If the wreckage was completely clear of the tracks, then they will just continue their transporting of materials.

The girl and I made it up the slight incline to where the old bookshop was. She perked up at the sight of the storefront. She remembered it. No doubt in my mind.

***

The next thing I remember was waking up to the sound of her voice—gentle and calming. She was having a conversation with someone I didn't know.

"I'm not being selfish. I saved him after all."

"You need... help." The stranger replied.

"That's not true. He saved me, so I was returning the favor."

"Awake." There was a slight buzz to the stranger's voice.

She turned to me, "Sorry to wake you. How are you feeling?"

I stretched and groaned. "All right, I guess," The sun was pouring through the dirty window, I squinted and muttered at it before I looked again in her direction. There was a transparent hologram standing before her—another woman. The hologram woman smiled. Her hair was cut short, shaved all the way down to the skin on one side while the rest of her hair combed down and away. "What is going on?"

The hologram looked away and said, "I should go." Then she vanished. A small box the size of a pack of cigarettes with a blue light on it, flickered out and the girl picked it up and stuffed it into her jacket pocket; the one inside that sat nearest her heart. At the train tracks she looked younger, but here in the new light of day I could see the age in her eyes. Not only age—the hurt that consumed her. She patted it once after it was securely inside.

"They were my partner," she said in a heavy voice.

"I'm sorry?"

She tapped the pocket again. "My partner. They took a job on one of those starships." She said the word with more disdain than I could ever muster. I was impressed.

"What happened?"

"The company said they failed."

"What the hell does that mean?"

The woman started crying. "I don't know. They were sent to find new worlds and I guess... Well, I don't have to guess. They told me she died," She waved the little object around, "This was the consolation prize. A shit hologram that is compiled of various instances of her on vid."

I crawled over to her and put my arm around her in a sort of half hug, not far from how we walked up the street. After a long moment, I asked, "So was last night an attempt to kill yourself?"

She shook her head. "No. No, not really. I want to hurt them. The company." She pushed herself away. "I want them to pay for what they do to people. I figure I can hide in this empty city and wage war on them until eventually they kill me."

I stared straight into her eyes. Her voice was clear despite the tears in her eyes. I didn't know what to say, so

I said the only thing I felt. "I'm glad you're alive." Only after I said the words did I feel that they were strange. I knew I should have felt bad but I didn't. I was glad. Happiness was surprising and felt like it belonged to someone else.

She stared into my eyes.

I didn't break from her gaze. Though I could see the sunlight soaring in around us. For once I felt warm but not from the sun, from inside my chest or my gut. I couldn't be sure.

"What are you doing here in this place all alone?"

I considered the question for a moment and then cautiously stood up, keeping pressure off my injury. I took in the room and how it looked so different now with someone else here. I hadn't really considered the why of it. I'd always made sure to avoid crossing in front of the windows so as to not see myself. I laughed and then I said, "I've been looking at it all wrong."

"How's that?"

"I didn't want to fit in with them. Well, that's not true. I did, once upon a time but that was before and that's where I've been trapped. Like this room," I spread my arms out, "You remember it too, don't you?"

She nodded. "I loved books."

"Me too. I've sat in here day after day, angry at myself... angry at that factory. But it isn't the place's fault. I was sad and angry and I brought that here."

She looked around and didn't say anything.

"This is where I need your help. What could this place be?"

"Anything," She shrugged, "it could be anything." There was boredom in her voice, faint but it was there.

"I'm thinking of one specific thing."

"What's that?"

I offered her my hand, "Let me show you." I raised her up and we walked to the door. "What do you see?" I pushed the door open and we walked out onto the sidewalk. I looked both ways and walked into the street. Spreading my arms, I looked into her eyes and said, "I always saw it as a dead city but it's not that."

She nodded. "It's empty."

"Waiting to be filled," I corrected.

The door clanged behind us, and as we made our way back to the tracks to survey the damage from the night before, I was surprised at how the sunlight didn't feel so bad. I even found myself looking up and marveling at how blue the sky was.

The empty storefronts we passed showed me something I hadn't seen in a long time. Two faces reflected back.

Under the Reign of the Sunlight King

Klipsa Preeda strolled through the entryway of the mighty throne room, her heavy boots clattering along the stone floors. As she drew closer to the center, her stride hardened and her body stiffened. She had a lot to live up to and nobody was going to take the responsibility or this status away from her; not after she tried so hard to prove herself to the Sunlight King and the greater population of the valley. Her selection was fairly unanimous. It still felt like too much.

She had spent the better part of a year campaigning—talking to people, explaining all that she was capable of. And now, she was here—outside of the Sunlight King's throne room. The whole place was warmer than she expected, and she expected it to be quite warm. After all, she was now one of the group called the Burning Men.

The heavy door to the throne room growled open and a slender figure appeared. Their head tilted to the side. Preeda noticed the visor the figure wore and immediately felt sweat bubble on her skin. This vaguely human shape was one of them—the Burning Men.

She swallowed and the shape slinked away like a long noodle with legs.

The door growled again and Preeda slipped in before it closed on itself.

The room was dark except for the shrouded light from inside the covered throne. Preeda knew it was more than just a seat within—it was a chamber meant only for the King. She stopped at the center of the room just outside the throne. Here the heat was even more intense as it permeated through the heavy curtain. The day was young and he was fulfilling his duty as King by providing light to the people of the valley.

"What is it, Guardian Klipsa?"

Preeda snapped her spine straight. "I'm your escort," She replied quickly.

"You've interrupted." The King bellowed.

"My apologies."

"Pull the curtain back and see for yourself."

Preeda froze. She did not want to see within, not so soon after he had released the daily light upon the valley. It wasn't for her to see.

"Guardian Klipsa, you have proven yourself worthy, and with that comes acquiring knowledge. If I had wanted another soldier, I wouldn't have selected you."

She swallowed and reached upward to the heavy canvas curtain. It was rough against her soft hands, which reminded her that she needed to see about acquiring gloves to hide her inexperience. As she pulled, she felt the heat from the King's light. There was a crackling noise and then a small jolt of lightning rose from below the King. She yanked the curtain the rest of the way and watched as the Sunlight King rose to his feet. He was nearly eight feet tall and his hands were bigger than Preeda's head. She held her ground as she gazed upon the giant. His chest was bare and she saw the price he paid to be King. His chest was charred and lined with lightning bolt scars. Some were scabbed over while others were open and bleeding. The only part of his upper body that retained a skin pigment like that of his face were his hands and half of his forearms, the rest of him was tattered with the price of harnessing light.

She had stood beside him once before, but that was mostly in performance at the close of her campaign. This was different. She became increasingly aware of the fact she was staring. He was smiling and she realized that they were alone.

"Your highness, I apologize for staring," She glanced down.

"Lift your head, you are no longer a peasant girl. You are Guardian Klipsa, *changer-of-the-tide*."

"*Changer-of-the-tide*? My King, you bless me with a title so soon?" She knew each of the Burning Men had a title but she wasn't sure what they meant. It felt strange, and she wished she could take the time to say it aloud herself.

The King pulled his multi-colored healing robes up over him, and he descended the stone stairs. "Walk with me, Guardian. We have the time," he said, rolling his shoulders beneath the heavy healing robes.

She started half a step behind him as they crossed toward the eastern balcony that provided a glorious view of the valley below. The struts of the throne room made it so they could look upon the residents. Directly below the throne room was a gathering place where people prayed and made offerings or just to bathe in the morning heat of the fresh sunlight. Preeda remembered it well. It wasn't long ago that she would accompany her mother to the warm prayers as she called them.

The Sunlight King turned to face Preeda and immediately she realized she was deferring to him still. She took the stare in stride and joined herself to his side. Again, she wished she could speak to herself and tell herself to get it together because she was changer of the tide, apparently.

They stopped at the balcony. The King stood with his large hands on the railing.

"Guardian Klipsa, I trust you know the story of how the first of my Burning Men came to be."

She nodded.

"I will admit it is strange having a strong relationship with a person that once vowed to kill me. The *all-see-ing-eye* is more than the first person to try to kill me, they have been blessed in a way I didn't know possible. The blue light is seen differently by different eyes. Which is where you come in. I look forward to what you find when you gaze upon the blue for the first time. I do not know what the future holds, but I'm well aware that nothing lasts forever. I'm going to be honest with you, Klipsa. The title *changer-of-the-tide* is not one that I understand, not in the way I understand the *all-seeing-eye,* but perhaps it has to do with your purpose for joining me."

The King looked out across the valley, the golden light of the day wasn't right and that was her fault, but it was her first day. Would he hold this against her?

"My purpose?" She asked.

"The story of how you are unwelcome is one to maintain my image. I do in fact want a woman here on my side. *As you saw, I am old, far older than I should be. As King, I know that change charges a heavy price. My hope is for you to ease my weary soul, it is lonely here with only the soon to be dead as my companions. I see us as equals, Klipsa though no one must know of our friendship. I hope this does not dissuade you from wanting to be by my side."*

Preeda shook her head. "No, my King. I'm honored." She nodded and watched as the King lifted a hand in a fist and rocked it forward once.

The King bowed to no one.

They continued to the palace room which was through the western entry and adjacent to the living cells of the Burning Men, which Preeda always thought of as the King's personal guard but being here... she felt different. Maybe it was the heat or maybe it wasn't. She thought it would feel like an honor to be the first person outside of the Burning Men to step foot within the stone palace. A tickle at the back of her mind pressed harder suddenly. She knew she was not outside of the Burning Men; she was one of them.

She had heard the stories but it was quite the sight the first time she gazed upon one of the Burning. When she was found worthy, after a lengthy campaign and designation process, the sixth Burning was destroyed. He was called *the-varying-guard*. Preeda understood this as an expression of how he was the first to actively campaign for a position. She knew at least the majority of the rest were failed assassination attempts where the would-be assassins got too close to the King and could never leave. The remaining five titles were unknown to her. *The-varying-guard* was reduced to ash after her acceptance into the palace.

The living cells were where the Burning Men spent most of their time. Preeda wasn't sure what they did to pass the time, but this was by far the most unsettling section of the palace. It felt confined and the only light was from the open doorway they came through. A shadow passed between her and the door, and the light was gone. Preeda tensed, causing her to hesitate. The King groaned and she rejoined him. Tiny lights started to blossom around them as they continued.

The hearts of the Burning Men glowed within their chests.

As they passed through the living cells, the Burning Men rumbled about the short duration of the day's lighting. Preeda shot them a scowl. Their snickering quickly turned to coughing as the proximity to the King increased. Preeda saw one of them cough a bit of smoke—the cloud passed in front of two glowing hearts. Knowing the source of the name was one thing but seeing the effects of their burning bewildered her.

She looked ahead of her and let her peripheral vision glide towards the King. How long until she too would burn?

The King smiled as he felt his Burning Men react to his presence. While most of them took to the burning well enough, there was one who Preeda quickly noticed was not like the rest. They were twitching and nearly seizing. She recognized the slender shape. They were the one she encountered earlier.

Along their visor, she saw glimpses of images. Too fast for her to process, as they were not for her.

The King motioned to them and Preeda crossed toward them, yanked them up and dragged them outside of the palace where they lowered their head but remained twitching.

"Report, all seeing eye." The King boomed.

The twitching ceased and the *all-seeing-eye* opened their mouth. "Alarm. The Dark Cliffs." They closed their mouth and pushed past Preeda back into the King's presence. The twitching stopped and a slight moan echoed throughout the room.

Preeda looked at the King who was grinning. They made eye contact and she knew she was going. She wouldn't be able to pull any of the other Burning Men away from their King. She walked to the nearest Burning and snatched his toolkit which wasn't much—a thick rope with a grappling hook at the end and a scraping of the Sunlight King's skin encased in a small vial which provided power to the Burning Men while they were away from him.

"Guardian Klipsa," The King bellowed as she headed for the entry.

She looked back and remembered what she had forgotten, with a slight nod she said, "The light of the valley shall endure."

The King repeated the phrase, his tone was indifferent. She didn't have time to consider what it meant.

Without further hesitation she hurried through the halls and exited the palace.

The Dark Cliffs were not far from the palace, she made her way quickly and efficiently. The temperature change was noticeable and immediately the little vial of the King's skin began to heat her to a temperature she was more comfortable with. How had it happened so fast?

The thought crawled around her skin and nestled in her mind.

She reminded herself she had a job to do. There was a threat to the valley and to the King, to her, near the Cliffs. She was all there was to handle it. She knew they used the word harvest in these scenarios but she knew it wasn't that simple. It was protection. She was in charge of protecting the valley and all who lived there.

This part of the valley was always her favorite—quiet and secluded. She was here earlier today thinking about everything that led to her being accepted in the palace. It was unreal. She gave up the life she had to be the first female in the palace. The light barely touched this area, only in little swatches and sunbeams and she loved it, especially when you saw the giant cliffs that extended straight up into the darkness. They started kind enough then shot straight up. Luckily there was a space flat enough to stand and get a footing to use the grappling hook on the steepest rocks.

She had to toss it three times in order to get it snug at the top of the cliff and still she wasn't sure it would hold. But she had a job to do. That job wasn't clear to her, but she figured it would be once she was face to face with whatever had tripped the alarm. The only thing she knew for sure was within the darkness lied something that was harvested by the Burning Men.

Preeda climbed the rope, struggling at first but eventually managing it just fine. The hook held and she was able to find something to pull herself up to the top of the cliff face. She stood in the darkness, trying to let her eyes adjust. They didn't. It was too dark.

A buzzing sound rose through the darkness. It quickly became more of a crackle and then there was light blue flash.

Preeda stepped toward it. "Is someone there?"

Another blue flash followed by a crackle. Then another.

"I know why you're here," The voice was small but confident. Perhaps strangest was how whoever was there spoke with a buzz to their voice, as if they were trying to imitate a bumblebee.

"Did you trip the alarm?"

The stranger scoffed. "Alarm? You really are something else."

"I'm not sure I follow. My name is Klipsa Preeda and I climbed up here to do my job."

"Harvesting. That's what you call it, yes?"

Preeda nodded.

"Do you know what you were sent to harvest?"

"No, but sounds like you do."

A louder crack and the blue flickering light brightened revealing a humanoid shape with skin lit with electric current. Immediately, Preeda thought of the blue lightning she saw in the throne room when she had interrupted the Sunlight King. She clapped a hand to her mouth.

"My name is Taffertilly, and I'm not going to die to maintain your way of life." The tiny buzzing voice matched the tiny buzzing body. She was the size of small toddler, only skinnier and she floated on little humming wings.

Preeda stood there, eyes wide, jaw hanging open, until she asked, "What?"

"It's written in the light. I guess you can't see it but I can. I've always known. I'm nineteen, and every day of my life I've seen the truth written in the sky. There are blue lines pointing toward the center of the valley. That's where it happens."

"The throne room."

"All I know is I heard my mother cry out last night and her light is there across the sky." Taffertilly gestured toward the sky, drawing a careful line above her.

Preeda gulped. "Does that mean..."

Taffertilly nodded. "Your people killed my mother."

"The procedure wasn't finished," Preeda thought of the scars on the King's flesh, "Oh, oh no."

"What?"

"I just realized that's why he looks—"

"My people don't take it lying down. We're taught to fight at a young age."

"How come I've never seen any of you before?"

"The people in the light are preoccupied. It's what my mother always said. Now, I guess I'll say it." Taffertilly looked toward the center of the valley. "You say it's the throne room?"

Preeda nodded. "The Sunlight King goes every morning and—"

"Kills one of my people. It's time someone turned the tables." Taffertilly stepped toward the cliffs and suddenly a burst of blue light emitted from her chest, and then she rode the lightning down to the valley.

"Wait!" Preeda yelled. There was a storm raging in her mind. If people knew the truth there was no way of knowing what would happen. She gulped when she thought of how it wouldn't take long for the King to know something went awry with her... harvesting.

Taffertilly was gone from Preeda's sight in seconds, and to Preeda's surprise the blue lightning remained in her wake. It was almost like a staircase. There wasn't time to waste, the buzzing of Taffertilly's movements were fading into the distance. She had to divert her before she too became sunlight. The thought chilled her to her core. With a breath, she jumped onto the blue lightning and she felt the current rushing through her. She was humming and buzzing and it didn't matter if she leaned one way or the other, her feet stayed on the track. In minutes she was on the ground, looking up at the blue. It was utterly amazing.

Feeling charged up, both literally and figuratively, Preeda ran faster than she ever had before. She was nearing the buzzing sound and just before the center of the valley was reached, she collided with Taffertilly, tackling her to the ground.

"You must listen to me," Preeda pleaded, "If you go there you will die."

"Then like my mother before me, I will die."

"Just slow down... maybe there's something we could do. Together," Preeda looked back up the cliff as the last of the blue faded.

The tiny girl with the blue aura smiled.

"What are you smiling about?" Preeda released her grip and pushed up on her hands, allowing Taffertilly to gather herself and stand opposite Preeda.

"I wasn't sure if you'd come down the light track, I laid for you. Glad you did."

"It does feel... great," Preeda said, almost surprised by her admission, "But I'm serious. You can't go to the throne room." Preeda felt the crowd forming around her and Taffertilly.

"Where then? People are noticing," Taffertilly's voice softened and within it, an ache.

Preeda swallowed hard. There was only one place they could hide while she tried to figure out what to do. "My mother's home isn't far." The words hurt. Preeda had given up on her whole life to join the King's guard. Which included giving up her mother. The word her mother last said to her shouted through her mind. Preeda swallowed and did her best to shake it off. It wasn't betrayal to make your own path.

Preeda scooped Taffertilly up in her arms and pushed through the growing crowd. The judgments were loud. The King would send for her. There was little doubt in her mind. She hoped she was wrong but she felt the end was near.

She ducked around a small building that was barely holding to its foundation. Resting against it, she looked at the small Taffertilly and she smiled.

"Try to quiet your light," Preeda whispered.

Taffertilly said, "I know. I'm trying. I'm scared."

Preeda realized that her worry may be passing to Taff. She had to push it all aside. "I've got you. Don't worry."

She hurried through the clay streets, slipping in and around the wooden structures until she made her way to where she had spent her first twenty-four years. A small wooden building, reinforced with mud and clay. Her family had rationed their water to ensure that their home had extra protection. She understood that it was because just prior to her birth, the Sunlight King had taken power and it was living through that time that inspired her father to give his life in service of protecting his family. As she passed his tiny grave marker, she patted it twice in quick succession. One for love and one as an apology.

With Taffertilly wrapped up in her guard robes, Preeda knocked on the front door. It rattled and the sound made her wince. The house was well reinforced, but it was old and there wasn't much to it.

The door creaked open and her mother was there, tears in her eyes.

"Tell me it's not true, Sasa," It was the pet name that was established when she was an infant. Her mother could never be broken of the habit.

"We can talk inside."

Her mother winced and held a hand to her mouth. "It's true. Oh, Sasa. I knew I never should have let you leave here. You never did understand your place."

"Mother, please."

"No, you endanger all of us. You endanger our way of life. Your father, rest his soul, spent his life protecting us and I had hoped you would learn to live similarly." She sobbed.

"Mother, I've done nothing wrong."

"First, you disobey and abandon me, then you disobey the King, and now you want me to welcome you in? No. Do your duty and bring that awful thing to the King. Word has traveled far that today is the shortest day because of you."

Taffertilly buzzed beneath Preeda's robes.

Her mother gasped. "Get away. Get away now!"

"Mother, please. I am begging you."

"No, you are a destroyer. You destroyed what was left of our family and now you wish to destroy our home. Be gone."

"But our lives are built on these people," Preeda opened her robes to reveal Taffertilly's face.

"They are foul creatures and deserve their fate!"

Preeda stepped backwards, shocked at her mother's words. "You know?"

"Of course. We all know the blue light makes way for our golden sunlight. We are rich under the Sunlight King's glow."

Preeda stood unable to move. She wasn't even sure she remembered how to move. How could everyone know? She thought of the houses she'd seen with little jagged marks throughout the roofs. It couldn't be.

But it was. Of course it was.

Lightning bolts.

She cried out as her thoughts walked her beside her father's grave and the bolt marks in the stone. Everything hurt and she felt sick.

"Give it here. I'll take it to the palace. I've done it before."

Preeda's mouth dropped open. "I can't believe you," she said and turned away from the place she once felt safest. Preeda screamed as she fell to her knees. She wanted to run. She wanted someone to tell her that it wasn't true.

Taffertilly buzzed inside the robes. Preeda got up and started running. She ran as fast as she could while still holding onto her new friend. How could she have come from such a selfish person? Preeda stopped and looked around at the shacks baking in the sunlight. Was it so bad before him that he is actually the lesser evil? She remembered his scarred flesh and the blue lightning.

No, evil is evil. But what could be done about any of it?

Everyone is fine with how it is.

Preeda growled in anger.

How could everyone be okay with any of this? She peeked down at Taffertilly. A warm feeling blossomed inside of her. Preeda was glad to have met Taff.

She knew what she had to do but she had no idea how to approach any of it. She had to return to the King, but then what? They were two and hardly able to take on the six Burning Men. The Burning Men were unpredictable and the *all-seeing-eye* would surely see them coming. It would be over before it even started. She couldn't even voice any of this because she couldn't be sure the *all-seeing-eye* couldn't see them at this point. She had no idea how far their abilities reached.

Who knew what other abilities the others may have. And surely if they came across any they'd want her dead so they could take Taffertilly back to the palace.

Taffertilly shifted around. "Someone is coming. Hide me somewhere. Quick."

Preeda found a tin bucket with a lid. It was turned over and soiled with mud but it would work. She moved it from against the shack just enough to get the lid open and placed Taff inside. "Don't make a sound."

Taff winked.

Preeda closed the lid and bent over, hands on her knees, across the street from the bucket.

Two tall men emerged from around the corner. They wore heavy canvas robes that constricted their movements. One pointed to Preeda and they approached her with haste.

"Return to the King at once," One of them bellowed while the other stood completely still. He didn't blink.

"Eventually, I will make my way there."

"No, you will go now! You have to. You can make this right." The first man shouted. The other remained motionless.

Preeda felt a spark of heat beneath her cloak. The one who held back must be the one she stole the vial from.

"Alive or dead, makes no difference to us," The Burning Man nearest her shouted.

She smirked and let it slowly turn into a laugh, as she produced the small vial from her coat pocket and threw the thing at him. It connected causing a chain reaction, setting ablaze the other vial hidden beneath the Burning Man's robes.

Their eyes turned flame red and in an instant their robes caught fire and were reduced to ash. Two Burning Men stood fully ablaze in front of her. The flames danced along their flesh in some places looking as though the skin was protected from the flame while in other spots like their shoulders were actively burning. What remained of their flesh oozed and popped. They each took steps toward Preeda and the sound of their flesh burning mixed with their groans overwhelmed her. Preeda was stunned, her senses overloaded. Even if she had another weapon, she wasn't sure there was anything she could will herself to do with it.

Sweat beaded and drenched her, forcing her eyes closed but she had to keep them open. She wouldn't close her eyes and die. She thought of her father and wished there was an answer hidden away in her memory. All there was were the two terrible creatures heading toward her. They weren't men. They were barely alive. To run away would be a defeat—they would die knowing they had won.

No. She stood and glared through her squinted eyes.

They were within reach. Burning flesh slipped off of their bones and landed on Preeda; all along her clothing causing it to quickly burn away, exposing her delicate flesh. She tried to duck away but it was no use. Their arms were only charred bone. Preeda was wearing what remained of their skin. The stench made her dry heave. And then it wasn't dry at all. She tried to wipe her mouth after, but there was gore all along her arms and she felt the heat of them on her face. She vomited again.

The two Burning Men joined hands and the flames grew as their bones grinded together. Their flames became one large fire, staring her down.

"We are *the-joining-flame*. The light of the King shall endure." They spoke together and laughed at the end of their joined statement. They laughed until all there was was ash and the stink.

Preeda stayed on her hands and knees for a while, breathing through the discomfort of vomiting repeatedly. Eventually, her heart calmed and she gathered herself, then retrieved Taff from the tin.

Taff looked at Preeda. "Are you okay? What happened?"

"I have to do something in the throne room but I've no idea what. The Burning Men have titles and the two that came for us had one title that they just fulfilled. I thought the titles were earned, but they are more like prophecies." Preeda stopped and wiped at the burn on her cheek.

"What was the purpose? They burned together. What a waste."

"It wasn't a waste. The Burning Men never leave the palace."

"What does that mean?"

"It means they defied the King and yet, their title still had to be fulfilled. Perhaps it would have been different, we'll never know."

Taffertilly squinted at Preeda.

"The King is waiting for me. I can feel it. He's going to kill me."

"How do you know?" Taff asked, her eyes growing large and nearly spilling off of her narrow face.

Preeda shook her head.

"See? You don't know."

"What is tide?"

"Huh?"

"My title. *Changer-of-the-tide*. I don't know what tide is."

Taffertilly shook her head. "We could go see the King and watch you fulfill your title."

Preeda sighed. "I'm afraid."

"I am too. Does that mean we should give up?"

Preeda considered the prospect. She thought about how she would feel to return to her role but then she saw herself standing in the throne room again, except this time the King's process was not interrupted and Taffertilly disappeared within.

She shook the thought away and tucked Taff under her coat. "There will be no giving up."

Taffertilly smiled and nestled herself snug within the coat.

Preeda looked ahead of them at the struts to the throne room, she would have to backtrack to get to the entrance. The *all-seeing-eye* would warn the King but, it's possible that's already happened and that they've already prepared for what was seen.

She didn't know what tide was, but change was something she understood.

"Taff, whatever happens inside, I want you to know I'm glad I met you."

"It's going to be all right. Right, Klipsa?"

Preeda looked away. Nobody waited at the palace, all was quiet. Too quiet.

"Klipsa?"

"This feels like the end."

"Why do you feel like that?"

"It's not fear. It's knowledge. I know nothing worth doing comes easily. My father taught me that." Preeda wished she could talk about all her father did and how she could never fully apologize for what she had done. He died keeping her from those that would recruit her for a strike against the King and here she was...

As she walked through the stone hallway, she saw the quiet curtain was down in front of the passage into the throne room. She did not know of a more perfect invitation. Preeda tore it down and gasped at what she saw.

The room was painted with the remains of the other Burning Men—ash and gore all over the room, from behind the throne came the Sunlight King. His robes were burned away. He had fought the Burning Men.

"You! You were supposed to be my confidant. You were supposed to be by my side. Have you come to your senses and are finally willing to complete the harvesting?"

"I do not serve you."

"If you are attempting to make me feel better, it's not going to work. Is that *the-joining-flame* I smell on you? I was wondering where they ran off to."

"Why would you kill them?"

"If you are *changer-of-the-tide* I—"

"Fear? You were afraid I'd turn them against you?"

The Sunlight King looked away from her and for the first time she saw him. She saw the hurt and the loneliness.

Taffertilly sprang from Preeda's coat and shouted, "YOU KILLED MY MOTHER!"

A buzzing sphere of blue light erupted from Taff shooting blue bolts of light in every direction. Two lightning strikes connected with Preeda and sent her flying to the other end of the room.

Several strikes rippled across the King's scarred flesh. The King howled. "Ha! Now this is going to be a fight!" He ducked his head and charged at Taffertilly who was floating in the air.

She conjured another sphere of blue energy at the King and it exploded in his face. Fresh scars rippled across his cheeks but he didn't stop. Taffertilly shouted for Preeda. "I used up everything I am. Please!"

The King snatched Taff out of thin air and held her in one of his mighty fists. "Do you see this Guardian? I want you to see!"

Preeda came to and rolled her neck, cracking the bones. She opened her eyes and saw the horror of what was happening across the room. She rolled forward onto her knees and saw something. There was a sphere below the throne, just out of sight. Preeda looked to the King and back to the sphere. As he moved and spoke, the sphere flickered. That was it!

He was harnessing the light of Taff's people and using it to create the golden sunlight for the valley. All she had to do was destroy the essence and he'd perish too.

She looked over to Taff who was squinting and trying with every bit of her to summon more energy to fight the King, but it was no use. They made eye contact and Taff nodded to Preeda.

She swallowed and made a fist then dove at the ball, fist first. It landed. Nothing happened at first—then there was a crack, then another.

The King screamed in pain, releasing Taff.

"You're a foolish girl. Do you really think it's as simple as taking their light?"

She knew from his reaction and from how the color in and around Taff had drained that the spheres were the source of power for the lighted beings. Taffertilly could never extinguish her light on her own but if Preeda destroyed the King's then maybe... Preeda hit the sphere again, in an attempt to speed up the process.

"My death will flood the world."

Taff and Preeda looked at each other, then the sphere split down the middle releasing a large burst of energy that collided and tore through Preeda.

Taffertilly screamed while the King used his last breath to laugh as rushing water echoed from somewhere not far off.

***

Though the valley wouldn't survive the oncoming flood, the final hours of sunlight were of celebration. Taffertilly made her way through the seat of the throne room and spoke to the people praying down below. Some listened to her, and soon everyone gathered under the last of the light provided by Taffertilly's mother. It was bright and glorious and Taffertilly was glad that the last shred of her mother's existence was accompanied by happy faces.

As the reign of the Sunlight King died, a new phenomenon came for those who lived in the valley. Heavy rains poured for days. The shacks collapsed before drifting away and people were struck down by the terrible flooding.

The house that Klipsa Preeda grew up in was the last to fall. Taffertilly floated above the water and watched as her friend's home was erased. She would remember all that happened here, and she would tell the tale of the people of the valley and how her people were used to provide a life for them. She would tell everyone who would listen and if they didn't listen, she would make them. The first female Guardian of the valley had many names, as was their way, but in Taffertilly's stories she would always refer to *the-changing-tide* as her savior, and most of all her friend.

She would often omit her friend's dying words.

"See? Have to be willing to wash it all away."

If they had an extra moment, Taffertilly would have told her friend: *Change comes every day. It's often small, like a chance encounter with a stranger that forever changes how I see the world.*

There's No Such Thing as Empty Space

Finn Redler rocked in the small seat of the escape pod as the rickety thing ceased with a violent halt. Peering out of the viewing slot in the heavy door, he gasped as a large piece of debris from the destroyed exploration vessel hurtled past. There wasn't time to save anyone but himself. The truth of his situation didn't do much to change the guilt. He slammed his head against the steel wall behind the seat.

"Headrest, not in the budget," he growled.

He opened his eyes, looked again at the vastness of space, marveling at both the emptiness and how he still felt the heat from the explosion. It was a ghost, all that remained were pieces of the ship he and his team were supposed to repair. There were five people on his team.

Khoury and Tramoro never made it to the large vessel, as they were held back to make sure their ship, call sign CR 06-033, had enough fuel for the return trip to Saturn. Blake and Winston were the forward team. Finn was meant to assist them but as he disembarked CR 06-033, he felt a shifting in the big exploration vessel. Then he heard the cascading explosions.

The escape pods were just inside their entry point and with no time to verify the pods were functioning, he hopped in Pod-02 of three with his team-mates' faces flashing through his mind. Their voices sounded like far off echoes. But they weren't far off, they echoed in his mind.

Two months ago, they were five strangers and it didn't take long to go from that to openly teasing each other over dinner. He wished he go could back to the previous night—what the ship deemed as night, anyway. The slop was the same, there was no changing that but he'd give anything to have that warm filth rolling down his throat as he fought back laughter.

Last night, they had chatted about the void—the great blackness, it wasn't serious of course. Winston was just having one over on his crew and it took a turn when Blake asked a question that usually didn't come up.

"Do you think there are aliens out there?"

Finn did his best to hold it together, but the others busted out laughing. All except Winston, of course. They had worked together previously, so it was safe to think that it had previously been discussed. Now that Finn was thinking about it, he realized it was a topic they were saving for just before a big assignment.

Shit.

The conversation was rational for a while until it wasn't. It was late and it was delightful, though no one could agree. It all made sense. Winston was good at what he did, the bastard.

He thought he should change his mind, what was the harm in believing in aliens? He wished he could apologize to Blake.

Guilt became hope in an instant, as something through the window in front of him caught his eye. Another pod! He saw the exhaust cease like his own and then there was a small fragment of debris that came shooting towards the pod.

They collided.

At first it looked fine, however Redler saw a tiny burst of air from the door of the pod. Presumably the viewport of the door, just like the one he was currently peering out of.

The pods are supposed to be rated and prepared for slight impacts. Another safety feature that the company skirted around.

The door of the pod flew off into the darkness of space. Redler saw Winston—his supervisor and mentor—ripped from within.

He stared out the viewport for a long time. How strange it was to go from a valuable member of a team to absolutely nothing. It was only a matter of time before he too ended up out there. It was where he belonged.

He sighed and glanced over the panels of readouts and moderate settings, not that any of them could control the pod—it was just a warning.

The temperature gauge drew his attention—it shouldn't be holding temperature; it should be dropping. He needed to know how long he had. He tapped the readout but the needle didn't move. Of course it was broken, why would the company spend money on proper equipment?

There wasn't time to test the pod before he hit the launch button. However, his first mistake was the choice to always remove his heat retentive suit before beginning on repairs. He ran hot and the suit just exacerbated the whole issue.

When he looked out the viewport he saw the massive explosions in a haunting afterimage. He reached down in front of him and tapped the temperature gauge again. At least the busted thing was occupying his mind away from the cold hard truth.

He was alone, and chances were if the company had a way of knowing the ships were destroyed then surely they would write him off as deceased.

If the heating system was damaged, then in order to diagnose—or maybe repair—its problem, he'd have to be on the outside of the pod. The company's needs didn't meet anyone else's.

The softer and less important point being he didn't pack his EVA suit. At least the pod provided plenty of oxygen to ponder his life.

Redler closed his eyes and thoughts of his departure date drifted along. It was something a lot of his colleagues discussed because it was one thing that everyone had in common. They had all left Earth. He had met some who had nothing to lose by joining either of the corporations hiring able-bodied people to explore the stars. The companies had mastered the sale of it.

For generations, people had imagined going into space and finally because of these enterprises spear-headed by obnoxiously rich men, we were able to fulfill the promise of our parents' parents.

Redler's family pushed him to go. He was nineteen and had no interest in a formal degree, not that that would have gotten him very far. As much as his mother wanted grandchildren, she knew it was a death sentence to start a family on Earth. She wanted what was best, and what was best in this case, was sending Finn into space in the hands of a multi-billionaire and their company. It was the easy choice, as the fires across the world raged and land disappeared into the oceans.

But Redler did not find love or family or even adventure among the stars. He found hardship.

In the escape pod, he unbuckled his shoulder straps that kept him fastened to the seat and rolled towards the system readouts. Everything was a-okay except for the damn internal temperature. It must have been damaged at some point in the life cycle of the large ship. And this far out, it was low on the list of priorities. This far out there was nowhere to escape to. In Redler's case, there was only a thing to escape from.

After hours of stillness, he was closer and closer to the end of his life. What a nothing life it was. Nobody would remember him. Soon, the Earth would swallow what remained of humanity, and then humanity would belong to the corporations—it did already but soon it would be indisputable.

He closed his eyes and was greeted by the nothing of his eyelids. Focusing on his breathing for a few minutes relaxed him enough to start drifting into sleep and just as his muscles went limp, the entirety of the pod shook as it collided into something.

Redler bounced around the inside of the pod until finally he gripped the tiny edge of the viewport with his fingers. He pressed his face against the reinforced glass and his eyes widened. Was that massive structure a ship? He only saw the part he was smashed into. He blinked and was able to make out intricate carvings along the sides of the structure. It was elegantly detailed and unlike anything he'd ever seen.

He clapped a hand over his mouth and stumbled backwards.

It couldn't be.

Intelligent life among the stars. He was at least a year away from Saturn and he had no way of knowing how far the explosion sent him. The escape pod was not much more than a coffin. The only thing to do was find a way onto the mysterious structure.

The pod rattled and Redler felt a slight buzz in his head, then there was the telltale airlock hissing sound outside the pod door. He watched as the door began to disintegrate before his eyes.

His mind flooded with panic at the idea of suffocating in the emptiness of space. As the last of the door vanished into nothing, he held his breath and braced himself for the pain to come.

Except it didn't. He instead felt warmth.

Whatever he had crashed into had first matched the atmosphere of his busted pod then it disintegrated the door. In front of him was a long tube that resembled aluminum foil in both sound and texture. He wondered if it would tear as easily.

He pulled himself out of the pod and floated through the tube as the artificial gravity of his pod wasn't mimicked—only the air. He floated through the tube careful not to touch the edges. He didn't want to tear his only way out of the casket.

At the end of the foil tube was a door that looked like it was looking at him. In the center was a small eye that blinked when he was near. Of course, he understood this was a sensor of some kind but Redler couldn't shake the resemblance to an eye. When it saw him, it rolled away like a giant stone, giving way to a dimly lit corridor. It was familiar enough. Though instead of the stark industrial nature of the ships he was used to, this felt alive. There was a slight motion to the walls and Redler became convinced that if he were to touch them it would be like touching the abdomen of a living being. It would rise and fall with the cleverness of breath.

He progressed through the hall, with his shoulders hunched forward and his head swiveling back and forth. He wasn't a soldier but he was doing his best impersonation of one. The hall ended and gave way to a staircase, Redler peered down it.

Darkness stared back.

He pressed his hand on the wall to his right to brace himself as he peered even further. As his hand touched the wall, it quivered. Redler snatched his hand back and glared at the wall. Something flickered behind him and when he turned, he saw that the lights in the hall were going out; starting at the pod and quickly going out one by one. The fast-moving darkness pressed on his heart and he committed to the stairs. As carefully and quickly as he could manage, he stumbled down the stairs in a clatter of heavy breathing and heavier feet.

Once on solid ground, he breathed deeply, slowly trying to gather himself. It was dark, no lights anywhere. And in the brief moments it took for his eyes to adjust, his fear was suffocating. He felt like he couldn't breathe. Soon, he would die and everything would be for nothing.

As his eyes adjusted to the darkness, he could make out the outline of a hall similar to the one he had walked down. Whoever built this was stuck on the halls too. It's always halls. He wanted to call out into the dark and hear what, if anything, would answer him. But the whole situation was still suffocating him.

He walked down the hall, careful not to get too close to the quivering walls. At the end of the long hall—he lost count at fifty-seven steps—there was a fork. He didn't want to choose; he wanted the ship to tell him which way to go.

Redler felt a smile form along his face and he chuckled at the idea of the ship telling him where to go. It wasn't true but, in a way, it was because things were designed a certain way. He took a breath. The air in that direction smelled better than the greasy scent coming from the right path. If there was someone here, they'd be to the left not toward the grease. However, if he were here to do repairs then he would choose the path on the right. His tools were lost to the explosion so he wouldn't be repairing anything. For a brief moment, he felt as though those days were behind him.

He chose the left path. The first few steps felt wrong, like he made the wrong choice but after a few more steps he started feeling right, even vindicated.

As he walked down the hall, he swore he heard the clang of his heavy boots on the usual metal gangway. When he listened closer, he didn't hear clanging because there wasn't any. There was no metal anywhere that he had seen. Slowing his pace, he listened to the sound his boot made when he lowered his foot down to the floor. It was a squishy wet sound. Redler shuddered.

Ahead of him, the air was turning sweeter and more attractive. It felt fresh and less like the recycled garbage he had been breathing since he left Earth. He'd heard rumors of ships with luscious oxygen gardens and he had hoped to see one but—

The lights ahead of him suddenly rose up, out of his sight line. He peered through the opening at the end of the hall and saw the lights continuing up. The room below was enormous. The two lights shot further up and then separated. One flew the length of the room which was at least twenty times the length of the ship he had been sent to repair. This was bigger than the old aircraft carriers the Earth's navy fleets used to operate. How could something be this huge?

Then he looked down.

Below him, the floor was made up of greenery. He saw trees and plants and all sorts of shrubbery that he knew all had names but he hadn't the faintest idea what any of them were. He struggled to process the idea that suddenly consumed him—how could something clearly so empty and hollow be also so full?

He felt small in comparison. Nothing ever felt so right—he was small in comparison. Who was he to breathe the oxygen provided by these beauties?

Something tingled and caused his neck to quiver. He was being watched. He had no way of knowing where they may be. The lights shone down, only revealing the greenery.

Still in the doorway, Redler scanned the room and saw no way of passing through. Neither above nor below. This place was not built for him. The weight of that thought made him feel heavy and unwelcome. When he turned, his face twisted aghast as the hall he had traveled down just moments earlier was now gone.

In its place was a singular platform hanging in the darkness. It was outlined with little blue lights, and was a mere half step above where Redler stood.

This platform hung there for him. He was certain and yet the truth bewildered him. Why would this be here for him?

The platform's lights flickered and rose slightly. He couldn't believe it. From the foil tube to the greenery and now this? It was all impossible. Everything had been rolled out for him and he'd never felt anything like it.

Someone wanted him to be here. He swallowed, and swallowed again, and again, until it hurt.

Welcome. Impossible.

It had to be a ruse.

The lights brightened along the edges of the platform and turned a warm orange. It drew him in. He always liked the color and wished it was used more, but he never saw it except along the edges of the industrial spaceships he worked on.

Before he knew he was doing it, his feet landed on the platform and he was being whisked upward into the darkness, into the nothing. He closed his eyes. His heartbeat quickened, he didn't know what lay ahead and it was nearly too much for him.

The platform stopped and shook slightly.

Redler swallowed.

In front of him was a small doorway that was perfectly his size. It looked just like the door that had slid away and welcomed him aboard the strange ship. He found himself thinking of it as a ship instead of a structure and that was surprising.

He passed through the doorway and was taken aback by the size of the room beyond. It made the other one seem small. How such a thing was possible escaped him. Wherever he was, it was more like a planet than a structure or a ship. Across the room, maybe four hundred feet from him was a thick fog. It clouded the air and made him feel sticky. He rolled his neck and the crackling sound echoed through the enormous chamber. It was impressive how such a small sound could fill the massive room. He took another step and the door behind him rolled shut.

He jumped.

A rustling sound emanated from the fog.

"Who's there?" Redler's voice crackled due to lack of use.

A computerized voice said, "Translating..." After a moment, "Complete."

Redler was about to speak when something moved again.

"Welcome! I am happy you are here!" A voice boomed from beyond the fog.

Redler didn't know what to say. The silence was thicker than the fog. There was nothing for him to look at, only mist.

"I have been alone longer than your people have traveled the stars." The voice changed from a thundering to a more conversational tone, though it was filtered through whatever computer system was translating it.

The mist moved slightly, in response to the voice. Redler quivered.

There was a loud crunching noise and a shadow moved behind the fog. A face bigger than the repair ship he traveled on emerged. It had deep set eyes and there was a little twirl to the end of the nose. The face looked more like stone than flesh, and the rest of the body crunched as it moved. The behemoth stared at Redler and then smiled, showing off long skinny off-white teeth. They looked more like skyscrapers than teeth, making the smile a city skyline.

"I was tasked with an objective but it is long obsolete. I do not need to be ambassador for a people that no longer exist. I suppose that provides me with perspective I cannot convey to you. I am the last of my kind." The voice was too loud, perhaps a tic of the software.

A long shudder traveled from Redler's lower back all the way to the base of his skull. His head rolled backward. Suddenly, he remembered he should be breathing and gasped.

The behemoth turned their head to the side. "Pardon me, are you in pain?" The voice leveled out and was more inviting; softer, like a bird instead of a storm.

Redler shook his head.

"Are you capable of speech?"

After a moment, Redler managed, "Yes," It was a fragile sound like a child's admission.

"My eagerness is a symptom of my long years of failure. After many, many years I have made contact."

Redler cackled and quickly clasped a hand over his mouth.

The behemoth turned their head the other direction.

"I'm sorry. I didn't mean to laugh. I—" He couldn't finish his statement.

The behemoth rose to their massive feet. The room trembled, sending shock-waves through Redler.

"You are the only human to look upon me. You are the only other living thing I have met in... your word is centuries."

"It doesn't matter if I'm dead," The words spilled out of Redler.

"Why does it not matter?"

Redler looked at his feet.

"The answer, please."

Redler closed his eyes and turned away. He took a deep breath. "I won't be recognized. Everyone must think I'm dead and soon I will be. This discovery means nothing if I don't live. Damnit, I sound ridiculous. I'm standing in front of a stone behemoth aboard a giant spaceship that seems to be bigger than a planet and all I care about is I won't be recognized for the discovery. Could I be more selfish?"

"You are a living being."

"What does that mean?" Redler snapped.

"It means you are alive and like you, I have experienced similar emotions. We exist. We occupy space."

The loud crunching of the behemoth echoed through the vast chamber as they lowered themselves down to face Redler.

"What is your name?" The behemoth asked, their voice lowered to a grinding whisper.

"Finn Redler, I repair ships," The words all came out together in a rush and Redler turned away, embarrassed.

The behemoth smiled their skyline smile, still inches from Redler.

Redler felt a slight burst of air come from the behemoth's mouth. "What?" Something moved in his mind. "Oh. The grease." He slouched.

"I have been trying to repair my ship for a long time. Perhaps you could assist me?"

He sighed.

"Finn Redler, you are not pleased. I do not understand."

"I don't know if you could under—wait, maybe you're the only one who would. I've done one thing my whole life and it's become so ingrained in me that I can't even introduce myself without appending it to my name. I'm talking to an alien, an alien who has been alone for centuries. Centuries," He said the word again, feeling every syllable, "I don't think that word is long enough." Redler sat down, staring up at the behemoth.

The behemoth didn't speak nor did they break from Redler's gaze. After a moment, the behemoth lowered further to meet Finn where he was.

"I want to hear about your travels. Will you tell me your story?"

"First, I'd really like to take a nap in your oxygen gar-
den."

The Redirection of Forever

Two people, two hearts intertwined; I wish I could say they'd never loosen but all things unravel.

You'll have to forgive me for sending these pieces one by one. I don't have much time, as I've already gone backward. And now, there just isn't any way to be sure the pieces will find you in their proper order.

Even if they find you out of chronological order, I'm sure you'll be able to piece it together.

She fell asleep as soon as her eyes closed because she knew the truth within his heart. When he said he loved her, his voice broke and swooned through a small but meaningful sentence. *We will be together forever.*

They were neither young nor old, but if you asked them, there were days when they felt one or the other. Middling is not a description anyone wished to use. Especially not Salek Proheda, for he favored only heights—never lows. Spending his days and his nights locked away in the lab beneath the home he shared with his lovely wife Gianna. Salek had trained himself to only need tiny bursts of sleep, understanding that the human mind was resilient and could be fooled in many ways.

Tonight, though he rose like he always did, she didn't tousle. She didn't have to mend the void by telling herself that she was married to a passionate man. Obsession was not a new trait; it was part of what she loved about him.

And maybe, just maybe, she was right to call it passion and not obsession.

In his lab, there was a peculiar organization method which many would refer to as a mess—once again, many men are fools but few believe themselves to be. Here in the center of this mess, we find Salek hunched over a new device.

***

"It should be working. Why isn't it working?" Salek slammed his fists on the table, rattling tools onto the floor. The flat, circular device stared back at him. He tossed it over, and flipping the rocker switch back and forth a few times, before finally leaving it in the on position; he turned the thing around and held it a few inches from his face. Nearly a mirror, he could almost make out his crow's feet despite the filthy fingerprints.

He sighed. "I'm not sure what you're supposed to do."

He pressed the switch and clanged the device onto the worktable, then bent down to return the mess to its rightful place.

If only he could consult the original creator of this unnamed device. Staring at the thing on the table looking more like a dinner plate than anything remotely useful, Salek knew he could trust the man who gave him the designs. Still, it didn't make any sense. Not the device. Not the designs. And sure as hell not the creator. He tried to shake the image of him and the multitude of questions that appeared in its wake. In <u>his</u> wake.

He stood and walked across the cluttered lab then paused briefly before returning. While he paced, he tried not to look in the direction of the thing at all. He thought about Gianna and how pleased she was earlier. The lie pinched at his heart and he stopped walking.

It was a mistake.

No, it wasn't, because a mistake would indicate a lie. She looked into his eyes and knew he was being honest. It wasn't just a way to get out of marriage counseling. It was the truth.

He started pacing again.

After several minutes of silence, he found himself spellbound by the round device on the table. He made it, yet it didn't work.

"Wait, how do I know it doesn't work?"

***

Gianna slammed the door behind her and dropped her purse on the kitchen counter. The days rarely went her way and this one was no different from the bullshit her boss rolled onto her to the prick that cut her off and then to come home to—

"Honey, are you okay?"

She gasped.

He was standing, hair a mess, and god knew what was on his face, but there he was, those big eyes locked on to her.

"I'm sorry for disturbing you, Salek."

"Nonsense. What happened?"

"The usual."

"Vincent Campbell, expert douche."

She nodded. "That's the one. And I know what you're going to say but, I like the job. Well, I like having the job. Having my own thing."

He crossed the small gap and took her in his arms.

Her emotions deflated and she just let him hold her. After a while, she asked, "Are you working on something new?"

He pulled back a little to look at her. "How did you know?"

"It's all over your face," Her head tilted to the side as she smiled.

He wiped and saw that she was telling the truth. Grime and dust caked his face, which had transferred to her clothes. "I'm sorry, dear."

"Don't worry about it. What's the new thing?"

"Um, I'm not sure. It doesn't have a name."

"What does it do?"

"Uh... I'm also not sure. It's a puzzle, I guess. I was... given the designs... anonymously. Yeah. They want to see if I can crack it."

"Any luck?"

Salek shook his head. "I should be able to test it later on tonight."

Gianna kissed a small spot on his forehead where there was no dirt. "You'll figure it out." She didn't love his sleeping habit or rather, lack thereof but she considered it passion. At least, that's what she told herself.

"Gi, there's something else I want to talk about."

"Yeah?" This was different.

He nodded.

"Can we talk over dinner? I'm hungry and you should get cleaned up."

"Sure, I'll have a shower and then dinner." He kissed her and started across the room.

"Any requests?"

"Whatever your heart desires!" He said as he turned out of the kitchen.

"That's not helpful!"

***

While Gianna slept, Salek did the unthinkable. He cleaned his lab. The last step was taking out the trash, which he saved until after the morning light struck through the large windows on the eastern side of the lab. The other side was protected from the harmful UVs, as it often housed any number of sensitive materials, the kind government agencies liked to commission.

When he returned from the brisk walk to the dumpster, which of course wasn't his choice but a small compromise to the immaculate state of the lot they lived on. Appearances are everything. It made it very easy for their house cleaner, Meral, who despised trash of any sort. Salek went as far as building an automated arm that sensed when there was a bag placed near the front of the dumpster and it would complete the rest of the task so Meral could avoid the dirty job. He'd been working on a voice command so Meral could run out and speak to the device but that was before Salek had a visitor.

The lab hadn't looked like this since they moved in. With a shameful sigh, he grabbed the mop from its resting place against the table beside the entrance to the lab. Salek exhaled and carried it up the stairs to the tiny closet at the top, just outside the kitchen.

Crossing the kitchen, he was struck by something. He turned back and gathered what he needed from the pantry, and then grabbed two eggs from the fridge. It took a few minutes to reacquaint himself with the flow of the kitchen but it wasn't long, nor uncomfortable. He caught himself smiling when he saw his reflection in one of the hanging steel pans.

With the omelet finished, he scrounged around the kitchen in search of the serving tray with fold-able legs. It was high up in the pantry. After momentarily considering the step stool, he wrestled the tray down without much trouble.

The thing was filthy and it took another minute to clean it.

"Shit, the food's gonna be cold," he muttered. "Let's get moving Salek."

Carefully, he laid the food across the tray and finished off with a cup of coffee. Sugar and cream on the side. He ascended the stairs, one by one. Every little movement jostling the mug of coffee, only then did he realize it was overfilled. Salek slowed in an attempt to maintain the integrity of what he'd made.

He turned the corner at the half way point of the staircase and swore under his breath. At the top of the stairs was a closed door.

"Easy does it. You got this." He whispered to himself before breathing in then out. He saw the door handle and smiled. Gianna insisted on the removal of all knobs in the house before they moved in. Salek always thought it was merely a cosmetic choice and now he's praising her. He turned to the side as he reached the last stair and lobbed his elbow up onto the handle. The coffee jostled in the mug, but none spilled. He realized he was holding his breath just as the door handle popped to let him know they were through. And as he pushed the air out, the door swung all the way open.

When Salek heard the spring, it was already too late.

The door swung back. Involuntarily, he swung his arms up, dumping the whole tray onto the floor in a cacophony of clattering utensils and shattered ceramic.

Gianna jumped straight up and screamed.

"I'm sorry, Gi!" Salek said as he knelt to gather up the mess.

"What the hell is going on!?"

"I made you breakfast."

When she didn't reply he looked up at her, still seated straight up and shaking. Her face was both bewildered and frightened.

"I forgot about the door," He looked back at it and realized the multitude of mistakes that had led to this point. He'd become an expert of leaving this room carefully and quietly. Salek turned back to his wife, certain that every word that came to mind, no matter the combination would be completely and utterly incorrect.

There wasn't much talk during dinner, Gianna saw something was troubling Salek, but it was difficult to broach such things. He would often jump down her throat, unprovoked. There was trouble down deep and she didn't know how to remedy it.

After they were both done eating, Salek took her by the hand and they went out to the deck that had a small place to sit, as well as a spiral staircase tucked in the corner that led right to their bedroom.

He opened the sliding door and encouraged her through then he slid it closed.

"Salek, you're worrying me."

"Oh, I don't mean to. I'm sorry. I just—outside is better, for this." He scratched the back of his head.

She faced him and took his hands. "You can tell me anything. I want you to tell me everything."

"I don't know how to explain it. It doesn't make sense. I've built this new device, and the man told me I had to tell you something before he would give me the plans. I agreed and somehow that was enough for him. I built the thing. I've got no idea if it works, but all the while I've thought about us. I've thought about everything."

He glanced away and to her it seemed like he couldn't bear to look away for long. She almost didn't believe it. His eyes were always so guarded and now they were open, pouring emotions onto her.

"Gianna, darling, I know we will be together forever because that's what I want." He sighed like the sentence weighed five hundred pounds.

She hugged him and they cried. The words played over in her mind, and she loved the little break in his voice between together and forever. It was everything.

She led him up the stairs to their bedroom and she fell asleep with her husband's arms around her. Gianna felt safe for the first time in a long while.

***

By now, it must be clear that I am lying. Whoever you are, you'd probably prefer I told this plainly, but after traveling and visiting Salek, my body and mind are in disarray. I must pay for the choices I've made.

Just know, I mean no harm. As I told Salek when I visited him in his lab.

***

He wanted to run to her and beg her forgiveness for the rude awakening but he felt too bad. He stayed where he was, frozen. Every dark night played over in his head; he saw himself rushing out of this room to get to where his work was. It was where he felt he needed to be. It was where everything made sense and if it didn't make sense then he could figure out why it didn't.

The device.

"Gianna," he said weakly.

She looked at him, still shook from being rudely awakened.

"I cleaned the lab. I wanted to bring you down there, but when I passed through the kitchen... I realized it was rude to wake you up and not have breakfast prepared." He paused, looking at the mess in between them. "And then."

"You cleaned the lab? And, you made me breakfast?"

He nodded.

"Are you okay?"

"Yeah, I think so. I mean, I was until this," he spread his arms to the breakfast.

Gianna watched his glossy eyes as he gestured at the mess that began as the most romantic gesture he'd made in years. He spent all night cleaning his lab to show her something. What was he working on? Something shifted in her stomach.

"Honey, what do you want to show me in your lab?" She couldn't hide the fear in her voice.

He got up in a burst. "It's not anything to be scared of. I just want to see if it works. I need your help."

Gianna didn't speak for a moment, instead her mind ran a flurry with all the years they'd been together and how he'd never asked anything like this of her before. She rose from the bed and extended her hand to him.

"Come on, then. Let's go see."

Salek looked up at her and smiled. He wiped his hand across his face, then across his pants before taking her hand, accepting her assistance in rising.

She led him down the stairs, leaving the mess where it was and they quietly made their way down to the lab.

The door pushed open with a hiss. When had he added an airlock system? She felt the clean air on her face. It was refreshing and instantly cleared her head. Inside, the lab was spotless. It looked like the end result of one of those commercials advertising some super cleaner. Gianna looked back at Salek who smiled his little half embarrassed smile. She reached her hand out to him and he took it. Together they walked, unimpeded to the focus of the room. A flat, round object resting on the table. It had loose wiring, and was clear to even Gianna's untrained eye that it was a prototype.

Salek said, "I don't know what it's supposed to do."

She stared at him, unmoving.

Salek took her hand and cleared his throat, "I know it's scary but I promise you, I wouldn't have you test it if I wasn't sure of the source."

"What source?"

Salek scratched his neck in an effort to look away.

"Okay. How does it work? How do I test it?" Gianna asked.

He cleared his throat and approached the device which lay innocently on the desk. "Easy. I think," He picked up the sides of the device and was instantly reminded of a steering wheel. "Hold it like this and I'll power it on for you. Easier that way."

"The power switch is on the back side? That's a—"

"Poor design?" He shook his head, "I hadn't really noticed before." He placed the device back down on the table and looked at his wife.

She smiled.

He watched her approach the work bench and look down at the device. She looked back at him.

"Where did you get this mirror?"

He pointed to the table on the other side of the room which had a round shaped hole cut in it. "I just scrubbed the hell out of it. It's a lot more reflective than I remember."

She smiled.

He thought she looked nervous and that made him nervous. But it had to be tested. It had to be. He couldn't explain it because it didn't make sense. Not a single part of it did. The stranger in the lab and the realization that the device's on switch was on its back. He had a hell of a time holding it upright and turning it on.

"How's this?" Gianna asked, peering around the edge of the steering wheel with a mirror in the middle.

"Great," he said, trying his best to be encouraging. "Are you ready?"

She nodded, but he could only tell by the slight move of the device in her hands.

"Are you nodding, Gi?"

She laughed. "Oh my god, I am so stupid. Are you sure you want me to test this thing? I feel very under-qualified all of a sudden."

"It's okay, Gi. You got this. When I power it on, just look into the mirror and tell me what you see. Okay?"

"Yeah, okay. I want to nod."

Salek laughed. Then he took a deep breath and pressed the rocker switch to its on position.

The steering wheel vibrated in Gianna's hands and she gasped as the surface of the mirror moved, like a single ripple from a lonely rain drop.

She blinked.

Staring back at her was her face, but wrinkled and tired. She wanted to clap a hand to her mouth but couldn't risk dropping the device. Distantly she could hear Salek speaking, but it all faded further and further away when the face in the mirror spoke.

"Some test, huh?" The older Gianna smiled. It was still her shining feature.

Present Gianna couldn't speak but was impressed that even in the future her smile remained as bright and powerful as ever.

"Hey, don't you worry, The Resting Bitch Face is still unmatched."

They both laughed in sync and Gianna thought it did look like a mirror for a moment.

"He won't be able to hear us as long as the device is powered on so you can speak. It's me, you know?"

Gianna looked at what appeared to be her future-self and smiled. "He really can't hear us?"

"See? He didn't react. I'm not sure how it works and I guess it doesn't matter, just that it does." There was a crack in her voice which Gianna first thought of as age, but it was something else.

"Aren't you worried that he'll hear you on your end?"

Gianna watched her future-self swallow hard.

"Oh. He... isn't here." The words sprang forth and consumed her mind. He wasn't there, but what did that mean exactly? Fear held her tongue.

The older Gianna forced a smile. "It didn't work out."

Four little words hit her like a runaway train carrying several tons of bricks. She couldn't imagine leaving him especially not now with his romantic side showing up.

"I'm sorry. You don't need to know all the details. Or any of the details."

"I... I just don't know what to say."

"You tell him it works. That's it."

"But wait, why didn't it work when he tested it?"

"It's best if you look around the side and tell him to switch it off."

"No, I'll decide what's best and I think it's best that you tell me what happened to my husband."

***

Salek saw the device shake and immediately he feared for his wife's safety. Flipping the switch to the off position, he took hold of the steering wheel. Once he had hold of the device, Gianna collapsed. Her hands falling immediately to her knees. He'd never seen his wife hunched over like this before.

He put the device on the work bench and carefully placed a hand on Gianna's back.

"Honey, are you okay?"

She took a breath and she moved so quickly; it was almost too fast for him to see. She went from bent over to squeezing him in a hug like they'd been apart for decades.

Neither of them said a word for a long time.

Curiosity finally got the better of him, "So, did it work?"

***

I realize this is a very inopportune moment to interrupt, but I have no other choice. Time is at my throat. These people are special to me and I feel somewhat guilty for misleading you. Here at the end of my life, I find that there is much nuance and far less black and white than I anticipated. For my whole life, I wanted everything to fit in these little boxes and have them all line up perfectly. The only things that line up are birth and death.

I would have told Salek this, but I thought it'd be more beneficial if I kept it short and gave him the plans for the device that could maybe redirect his life. I don't want him to make the same mistakes I did. By now, it's probably obvious that he and I are the same. Our births line up, but few other things do until the point just before I stepped in from my time —or perhaps it's that moment that separates us? Either way, I showed him my face after giving him the plans and he asked the one logical question anyone could ask in that moment.

"Why should I trust you?"

I think it's fair to say most people when faced with their future-self would trust what they had to say. Though, if I was in that position I'm not sure if I would trust a future version of myself.

Simply because of what I'm about to do.

I had not expected the traveling to enact irreversible damage to my body, and as such it's left me with no other choice. I thought, foolishly, that two Salek's could repair their love stories in parallel.

I'm sending this suicide note backwards in the time stream and when she enters the half-opened door of my lab, she will see me on the floor and the strange steering wheel device humming on the table. It's my one regret. I don't know for sure, but I think it's the same for her as it is for me. We loved each other and that leaves a mark. It's not as simple as wishing I could tell her everything. It's more complex than I know how to put into words, but I did find two words that seemed to do well by the meaning. They weren't planned. They just came out when I spoke to my younger self. It just happened.

I think that's what truth is.

It doesn't need thought. It doesn't need preparation. It's just there.

I wish she was here.

***

Gianna wanted to fight the tears, and for a moment she did, until the dam broke. Hearing her future-self struggle through the words and the tears as she described what was there in the lab, it was all overwhelming and holding her Salek was the only way to keep the image away.

He asked her the little innocent question.

"So, did it work?"

Her whole body trembled. She squeezed him harder. How could she tell him?

She had to tell him.

"I... um, I think so." She said fighting through her tears.

He shifted.

She felt him wanting to pull away and look at her but she wasn't ready.

"I have to—"

"Gi, I have to tell you where I got the designs from."

"It's okay."

"No, I lied. I'm sorry. He told me I had to tell you that we'd be together forever. He said it had to be those words. When I said them, I don't..." he shook his head. "No. I know I didn't mean them. It's been bad and I don't know if I can make it work."

He deflated in her arms. She squeezed him and then leaned backward to look at him. "Listen to me, I saw myself in your machine. A future version of myself. Totally unreal. We talked. She was here in the lab. She hadn't been here in a long time because they couldn't make it work. But the way she talked about... him." Her eyes drifted from Salek. "It wasn't over. And for him, it wasn't over either. I think what they wanted to tell us was love doesn't end. He died to tell us."

"I... he died?"

Gianna nodded.

There was a heavy silence and then they embraced.

Salek pulled away, his eyes wide. "That's it! He was trying to show me my future."

She shook her head, "I don't understand. You said it didn't work."

"Right, it only worked when I gave it to you."
She smiled.
A tear rolled down his cheek.
She leaned in and kissed him.

The End.
But not for them.

Afterword

Thank you for reading.

I really do appreciate it and by all means, if you have thoughts you wish to share, you can reach me via my website: https://edwardkane.net

I want to take a minute and thank some people that helped me along the way.

First, to my lovely wife, thank you for everything. From all the dinners you've cooked while I tapped away at the keyboard to all the silly conversations about dumb story ideas, and all the bad stories you've read over the years. I love you.

To Dan, I had no idea that joining up with GateCrashers was going to change my life but it has. Thanks for all the support and encouragement!

And to everyone else at GateCrashers, y'all are the best!

Extra special thanks to Scott Snyder for being a tiny part of the inspiration behind this collection. He read the first story, and the things he said about it were genuinely a massive boost—the first domino that led to publishing this book.

And a special thank you to all the people I can't possibly list that read some of these stories (or other ones I've since abandoned). Just because you aren't listed, doesn't mean you aren't important.

Huge thanks to my editor, Devin, who has become a friend and a great source of inspiration.

Extra special shout out goes to my friend Stipan Morian! Not only for his excellent art he contributed to this book and my Kickstarter campaign, but also for his kindness and vote of confidence.

Thank you to all 67 backers of my first ever Kickstarter campaign! They didn't just kickstart a book, they kickstarted my career.

One more note to end on before you close this book.

It feels a little strange to look at all these stories together, so much of this is in direct response to the pandemic. A few of them predate COVID but a lot of these wouldn't exist without the experience of living through the pandemic. I don't want to harp on this too much, but I want to mention it. I very nearly published a short collection of stories (some of the ones here) in March of 2020.

I'm glad I didn't.

It's been a hard few years and this year is no different, but my writing is better for having lived through the pandemic. I don't mean in a "starving artist" sort of way. I'm a more empathetic person and far more emotional. I don't actually know if it comes across in the stories, maybe in some of them but I can see the difference in me as a person pre-pandemic versus now.

Lastly, I just want to acknowledge the fact that I did a thing that I've been talking about and dreaming about for so long that part of me wasn't sure I was capable.

I can dedicate a book to myself and I sure as hell can thank myself at the end of it. So, thank you to me, both past and present. Can't wait to see where we end up next!

And you, *dear reader*, I hope you're kind to yourself today.

What's the thing you've been wanting to do?

-Edward Kane

October 2024